T0023375

interrogate both the rigidity of movements and the complacency that can find its way into them."   —Kristen Martin, *The New Republic*

"Blasting easily woke platitudes, this honest, hilarious, and deeply healing novel gets at the heartbreaking core of building connections between families and friends, and solidarities within and between racial communities. For years I've been waiting for a novel like Ryan Lee Wong's *Which Side Are You On*, and I urge everyone to read it. It is an astonishing debut."   —Cathy Park Hong, author of *Minor Feelings*

"Salty, funny, angry, and heartbreaking, *Which Side Are You On* synthesizes the struggles of a family that has been working and hoping for a better world for two, maybe three, generations, and in the process, renews our sense of the histories involved—American history, Korean American history, Black history, Los Angeles history. This is a stunning debut, but also a novel I didn't know I was waiting for."

—Alexander Chee, author of *How to Write an Autobiographical Novel*

WHICH
SIDE
ARE
YOU
ON

WHICH SIDE ARE YOU ON

A Novel

RYAN LEE WONG

Catapult
NEW YORK

Copyright © 2022 by Ryan Lee Wong

First Catapult edition: 2022
First paperback edition: 2023

Hardcover ISBN: 978-1-64622-148-6
Paperback ISBN: 978-1-64622-202-5

Library of Congress Control Number: 2022933780

Cover design by Gregg Kulick
Cover images: sign © Getty Images / donald_gruener; city © Shutterstock / StoopDown
Book design by Laura Berry

Catapult
New York, NY
books.catapult.co

Printed in the United States of America

10 9 8 7 6 5 4 3 2 1

엄마

WHICH
SIDE
ARE
YOU
ON

I

I SPOTTED MOM WHITE-KNUCKLING
the wheel of her Toyota Prius toward the curb. The car was new: Mom
had finally broken her lifelong boycott against the Japanese colonizers
because, she explained, the mileage was unbeatable, and anyway, we had
to let go of that ancestral shit sooner or later.

A massive concrete belt shaded the arrivals area at LAX. The air was
hot and tasted like dust and metal. A sea of black rideshares honked and
jockeyed for space while the passengers around me squinted at their
phones trying to match the cars to dots on their screens in the neoliberal
perversion of hailing a cab.

Mom leaned out of her window, grinning and flailing an arm. Her
car drifted forward and a rideshare driver let loose his horn. He turned
around and thrust his hand up rudely.

A cold dread rose up in me. I knew what was coming.

"Hey, motherfucker!" Mom's scream was like a gunshot and her
smile disappeared into a grimace.

The man stared, frozen in an awkward pivot out his window.

"Don't honk at *me!*" she yelled. "Watch where you're going."

The man shook his head, almost somberly, and sped away. A few others turned to stare, Mom's voice having risen above the commotion and roar of engines, and kept staring as they realized it had come from a round-faced, middle-aged Asian woman with a sensible bob.

Mom double-parked, and by the time she got out she was wearing a big, childlike grin again.

"My son!" she exclaimed, wrapping me in a hug. "What," she stepped back and looked at me, "you're embarrassed by your mother? Please. English is my second fucking language."

"I mean," I muttered, "your car *was* rolling forward."

"I must've been distracted by my handsome son." Mom reached out to smack my cheek with the butt of her palm, that babying gesture I knew from childhood.

I rolled my eyes and stepped back so that her fingers grazed my face. I slid my carry-on into the trunk and, before the traffic cop could scold us, climbed in and shut the door with a thump. The din of the arrivals area evaporated, replaced by the soft whisper of air conditioning.

"How is Halmoni?" I asked.

Mom was silent.

"I could've come back sooner."

"I told you about the surgery," Mom countered. "You said you were busy with all the organizing."

I didn't remember that, but she was probably telling the truth. I usually scrolled through Twitter during our phone check-ins as Mom ran through her list of updates and Dad interjected with the occasional joke.

"Yeah, well," I said. "It's a critical time—I might miss the sentencing."

"Wah, a serious activist!"

Mom and Dad talked about my activism with the same condescension other parents talked about their kids' singer-songwriter careers. "Pickets in Brooklyn are no joke," I said. "We have to stomp so our toes don't go numb. It's not like protests here, where people wear shorts."

"You're gonna freeze your skinny butt off," she chuckled. "I think about you whenever it's in the paper, that Chinese cop. You can tell from his face that boy's a little lost."

"Yeah, he was probably 'lost' in that public housing stairwell; 'lost' those twelve minutes he waited to phone dispatch, while Akai Gurley lay bleeding from the bullet he fired."

"Reed," Mom's voice dropped. "All that activism is making you harsh."

I thought back to when I'd first seen Peter Liang in the courtroom. We all wore head-to-toe black in solidarity with Akai Gurley's family, his partner and daughter and aunt sitting silent and upright a couple rows in front of us. The bailiff brought in Liang and I leaned over, wanting to look the killer cop in the face. But Liang's baby cheeks and dumb-founded expression, his somber navy suit and basic East Asian haircut, only reminded me of the kids I knew in high school: B- Asians who always lagged a beat behind, sold weed, and asked to copy my calculus homework. I felt, of all things, let down.

Mom's car passed through the Inglewood oil fields, a wasteland of scrubby bushes dominated by a silent army of pumpjacks churning up the earth. They dipped their insect heads until counterweights swung them back up.

"They're going like we don't have a hole the size of Antarctica in the ozone," I said.

"That's why I got this Prius," Mom said with pride. "You know it gets fifty miles a gallon?"

"I guess that's a Band-Aid solution."

We idled at a red light and Mom punched a button on her armrest. The locks clicked open. "You could always walk home."

I turned my head and caught a flicker in Mom's eyes. She let loose her big, guttural laugh that finished with a little cough-wheeze.

"Okay, you got me," I said.

"Ai, so serious," said Mom. "You're reminding me too much of myself back in the day."

* * *

Halmoni lay on a hospital bed staring at me as if I were a stranger. I almost didn't recognize her, either: The hair she'd permed and dyed black all my life now grew in a gray shock. Her face was puffy and the mischievous glimmer in her eyes was gone. I'd never seen anyone look so helpless.

Mom and I sat next to each other in plastic chairs. "Maybe it would've been better if she'd never come to this racist country," I said.

Mom turned to me and arched her eyebrows. "Her husband was a dog and her life in Korea was shit." She shrugged. "It's not like she had much choice."

"You mean your father. Was a dog."

"He wasn't a father to me." Mom clicked her tongue. "Halmoni, for that matter, wasn't much of a mother."

She leaned an elbow on the back of her chair, where her big, red "Goyard" purse hung. It was a top-rate Korean knockoff and she'd challenge anyone to tell the difference. She'd worn her nice leather jacket, too, as if to say this Koreatown care facility—the buzz of television from the next room, the thick bodily smells, the metal blinds—couldn't touch her.

"That's a little harsh, considering," I said.

"What, I'm supposed to be nice because she had a stroke?"

"Traditionally, yeah," I said. "This is a time of reconciliation?"

"I got her a nice bed, close to the window, and I brought flowers." She pointed at a lavish purple orchid sitting on the nightstand.

Halmoni gummed her lips as if to protest but only managed to show us a handful of bottom teeth. I tried seeing the room as Mom did but couldn't get past the tubes dangling from under Halmoni's hospital blanket, one of which hooked into a feed bag that whirred and slid an inch of goop into her. "Nice," I lied. "But does it count if you do it so grudgingly?"

"Ai, my smartass son," she said. "You don't know the shit I put up with from her."

"No, I don't. You've never told me." I had some very basic questions about this frail woman lying in front of me that I'd always meant to ask in the future, when my Korean was better. That future was gone now. My Korean was still crap.

Mom flopped her hand in a lazy circle, dismissing my challenge.

A man knocked and strode—a little too familiarly—into Halmoni's room. He wore a black smock with short sleeves and beamed. I thought of the Korean Christians in high school who walked with me to the bus stop, invited me to their Sunday morning "concerts," and expressed sincere concern for my eternal soul when I declined. The man spoke to Mom in Korean, something about *Her son? So handsome*, and mentioned Chee-chush, the savior. I smiled, tight-lipped.

He took a small black jar out of his bag, screwed the top off, and dipped a finger inside. He rubbed the pearly lotion into Halmoni's cheeks as her eyes swung around the room. I stared at this man touching my grandmother's face—something I hadn't done since I was a baby.

"He comes every week to do this for the patients," said Mom. "Nice, huh?"

"Mom. This is obviously a last-minute attempt at conversion."

Mom relaxed another inch into her chair. "Look. She loves it. She would've accepted a facial from a Buddhist monk, too."

"Religion is the opiate of the masses."

"Then Halmoni would've smoked it," Mom sighed. "It's ironic: In a way, this is what she wanted. To lie around all day being taken care of."

The pastor screwed the lid back on his jar. Halmoni shone like a waxed apple. He stood up and handed us each a pamphlet. Mom took hers and pretended to study it.

"Ah, no," I said, waving him away.

Mom jabbed me in the ribs. "Are *you* gonna give Halmoni her facials?"

I took the pamphlet and mimed interest in the haloed dove soaring across the cover. The pastor beamed at me. I watched him leave, then crumpled the paper and chucked it into the hamper full of used wipes and latex gloves.

The air in the room felt thinner, and I squeezed my eyes shut. I was five and watching Mom hold our old landline in the hallway, back when phones were plugged into walls. She yelled in Korean, her eyes drawn wide until she slammed the receiver down with a harsh clack of plastic on plastic.

"Remember," I said, "when I was a kid, any time you were on the phone with Halmoni, I'd yell, '*Talk nice, mommy! Why can't you talk nice?*'"

I opened my eyes. Mom's jaw was limp as if she'd been caught in some guilty act. It was a rare moment that showed me how, the rest of the time, she weighed each emotion inside before letting it surface. This face was innocent, unguarded, and I knew she hated anyone seeing it.

She forced a cough. "I was probably telling her not to spend her money—my money, that I sent to her—on those goddamn stocks her fortune-teller told her to buy." She pursed her lips, inviting me to counter.

I looked instead at Halmoni, who'd been following our conversation, her head rolling back and forth on her pillow. Halmoni and I had shared no plates of cookies or heart-to-hearts at the kitchen table. Her main shows of affection were inappropriate birthday gifts, like the stack of scratch-to-win tickets she handed me when I turned six. I dug up the shiny squares with a penny and jumped with excitement when I won five bucks. I begged my parents to let me redeem it while Halmoni grinned and Mom clucked with irritation.

"Obviously I don't agree with her materialism," I said. "But clearly Halmoni was deprived of something, and expected to get it back through this American fantasy of hitting the jackpot."

"Excellent analysis, my son," said Mom. "Materialism—that reminds me." Mom reached into her Goyard bag and pulled out a box. "Halmoni doesn't have a will or anything, and there's nothing to give you. But you could take this."

I opened the box. A small teapot and four cups shimmered in the dim light, white porcelain glazed in a lush blue. A golden chrysanthemum bloomed on the teapot, its petals outlined in fine metallic thread.

"Halmoni would buy all these beautiful things," said Mom, "and when I asked her why she never used them, she'd say she was waiting to move into a big house—hint, hint—where she'd have a china cabinet to keep them all. So they've never been used—how silly is that?"

I felt a little flurry of greed at the luxurious set, as if it whispered that a cleaner, more beautiful life was possible. I shut the lid and handed the box back to Mom. "What," I sneered, "I'm going to serve fine jasmine tea to my activist friends, to go with our cheese popcorn?"

Mom groaned. "My mother wouldn't use them until she had a mansion and my son won't because he's waiting for the revolution."

"I can't believe you're comparing Halmoni's class aspirations to my activism."

She shrugged. "They're both fantasies."

"You know," I said, "other Asian American organizers are always amazed that my parents are political." I pictured the way my friends' eyes lit up, then went gloomy as they talked about the cold standoffs they had with their own parents, who threatened to stop supporting them unless they went back to premed. "Then they ask me these questions that I can't answer because you and Dad never talk about your pasts. It's like—you won't pass down what you learned, and yet you think our analysis is naive. So maybe," I calmed my voice, "you could actually tell me? Help us build cross-generational activism so we're not starting from scratch?"

"Oh, all that ancient stuff," Mom murmured, like I was being tedious.

Her phone dinged. She slid it out of her jacket and punched the screen with her index finger in that awkward way boomers did. "Looks like Dad can meet us for dinner. I bet you miss Korean food."

I was thrown by the quick shift.

"Good," she said. "There's this new barbecue place on Vermont. All my K-Town friends say it's the best."

"You're just going to dodge my questions?"

"Who can talk about these things on an empty stomach?" She stood and shrugged on her big purse. "Say goodbye to your halmoni."

The sky was darkening outside. The fluorescent boxes set into the drop ceiling buzzed on, searing everything in a blank, shadowless light. Halmoni stared at me with watery eyes as if, though she hadn't spoken, I'd missed everything she'd tried to tell me.

II

OLYMPIC BOULEVARD WAS JAMMED with rush hour traffic. Mom's car would crawl forward ten feet only to stop and rock us back into the fuzzy seat fabric, a rhythmic motion that, with the whisper of sixty-eight-degree air conditioning, numbed me into a familiar stupor. I felt my mind atrophy into the naive contentment it had known before college, all my hard-learned analysis drying up like the L.A. River in a drought. I looked out the window for stimuli, something to pinch me awake.

The sky turned a glum purple, silhouetting all the unremarkable buildings lining the boulevard. Hangul signs advertising noodles, dry cleaning, and tax help went dim while the neons of restaurants and drinking houses lit up for K-Town's second shift.

"There's something honest about the way capitalism operates here, where they don't try to dress it up in grand, shining buildings," I said. "Just plunk it down in a strip mall and hang a sign."

Mom laughed. "This is what's going on in that big head? You need to get out and move, stop thinking so much." She roughed up my hair as if to shake loose my thoughts. "Who cut your hair?"

"My friend Tiff. We were experimenting with noncapitalist hangouts, where instead of going somewhere to buy something, I helped them hang a shelf and they cut my hair."

"No wonder it looks like shit," said Mom, feeling a lock between her fingers. "I hope the shelf you hung isn't this crooked."

I blushed. "God forbid the dead cells on my head don't conform to normative beauty standards."

"There's beauty standards, and then there's"—she tried to smooth down the sides of my hair—"this."

I shifted away from her and hit my head against the window with a little *clod*.

Mom clearly preferred my basic, liberal, professionally bound freshman friends to my activist ones. I could never explain to her the aura that surrounded these new friends, something I hadn't known existed but that made my previous goals—honors societies and prestigious summer internships—seem boring and conventional. Tiff cut their hair punkshort and wore thick, black eyeliner and red lipstick. Ash let one curl, dyed a neon green, poke out from her beanie and wore a T-shirt that said ASSATA SHAKUR IS WELCOME HERE. The two of them held hands on campus, wearing practiced faces that showed that they both enjoyed and disdained the stares they attracted. This was before Black Lives Matter made being "radical" "cool," when it was almost mandatory to be an untroubled liberal. Taking a flyer from Tiff or Ash, even standing too close to them, felt dangerous, as if they emitted a perfume that clung to you and marked you as an accomplice.

I was in Chinatown with a friend one night when Tiff met us for hand-pulled noodles. They'd just come from a tenants' rights meeting and buzzed with energy, holding forth between slurps on issues I didn't know I didn't know about: the tenure battles of faculty of color, Columbia's investments in Zionism and mass incarceration. They joked about confronting white kids about race with the goal of getting them to blush from anger, a game they called "roasting marshmallows."

I mostly nodded and offered monosyllabic affirmations, hoping they couldn't tell how little I followed. They didn't address me directly until the end of the meal, when I ordered a second plate of noodles to take back to the dorm for later. They grinned and said that was "incredibly fucking Asian" of me, then did the same thing.

Tiff was, perhaps, too much like Mom herself back in the day. What was the point of going to an elite East Coast school if I just ended up befriending a bunch of activist immigrants?

Mom's Prius trudged up the hill toward Koreatown Galleria, a gleaming monolith that could've been in the middle of Seoul. Huge banners showed pale, surgically double-eyelidded women holding credit cards and perfume bottles, as if showing how well Koreans had learned the consumerism and beauty standards of the people who had invaded them.

"Since I'm working from home more," Mom said, "I'll take you to my stylist to fix that mess on your head. My friends swear she's the best in K-Town. And we can go for yoga or hikes in the morning."

"It feels weird to be doing aerobics when I came to visit my dying grandmother."

"Ai! That's my whole point: you have to learn to take care of yourself, so you don't end up like that."

"Wow," I said. "Anyway, 'self-care' has been so co-opted that instead of a radical assertion of personhood under racist capitalism, it's come to mean the opposite: sipping matcha lattes and paying twenty-two dollars for yoga classes to perpetuate companies branding that lifestyle."

"We'll see about that," she said, as if I'd just challenged her to a contest.

Mom pulled into a strip mall. Of course the best barbecue in L.A. would be in a two-story cement structure with a pool hall stacked on top of a laundromat and a phone repair shop. A man in a red valet vest stood in the lot and flapped his arms at the unruly customers maneuvering their Benzes.

Mom stopped the car and tossed the valet her keys in a smooth way that showed she was a regular. I followed her into the restaurant. The entryway was covered with photographs of the owner posing next to the Korean celebrities who'd eaten there, all mediocre images snapped on a phone then printed and framed.

"You know any of these people?" asked Mom.

The celebrities and their radiant skin and multicolored bangs— though I hated to echo the orientalist phrase—all looked the same. "Not a single one."

The maître d', a woman wearing a headset and slim, black clothes, came over, smiled, and rushed us to a table. She could've been in one of those pop groups on the wall. This was not one of the Korean restaurants of my childhood, where cranky ahjumas in hanboks did everything with an edge of condescension, and you had to ask for extra panchan with the right amount of deference or they'd groan with the weariness and resentment of a sick relative.

LED lights shone on all the tables, illuminating the sizzling meats and just-washed lettuces. Green soju bottles gleamed as businessmen poured each other drinks. Dad waved at us from a corner. He wore one of his dozen nearly identical gray suits that Mom called "of the people" and always threatened to throw away in exchange for something more stylish. The only thing stopping her was understanding that it wasn't appropriate to dress "too well" in the labor movement, where compared to the others, Dad was practically chic.

Dad got up and we embraced. The two of them pecked each other on the cheek, then sat down across the table from me, the usual position, as if I were up for an interview.

"How did Halmoni look?" asked Dad, while Mom scoured the menu. Neither of us bothered to read it; Dad, the dutiful Chinese husband, and I, the illiterate halfie, had no say in the task at hand.

"Bad?" I said.

"It's because she can't get her hair permed," Mom interjected.

"I'm sure she appreciated you visiting," said Dad.

"Yeah. I don't think she recognized me."

Mom pushed the small brown button on the table to summon a waiter, the button at every K-Town restaurant precluding the danger of drunk Koreans sitting too long without service. A young man, his hair permed into wavy bangs, appeared immediately. Mom stated our order, no pleases or thank-yous. He bowed and was gone, having spoken all of three words.

"You ever notice," I said, "how you're never nice to the waiters in Korean restaurants?"

Dad chuckled. "*Talk nice, mommy!*"

"I'm older." Mom shrugged. "It would be weird if I were too nice."

"In white-people restaurants," I said, "you make conversation with the waiters."

"That's because they're so sensitive. If you don't say, '*Hiii*, how was your *day*?' they get all grumpy."

Dad and I burst out laughing. Joking about white people and their sensitivity had gotten us through some bad encounters on family vacations, in high-end restaurants and stores. I got to college and learned to call it a survival strategy against white supremacy.

"I restrained myself from asking Reed all the basic questions," said Mom, "so he wouldn't have to repeat himself for you."

"Being married so long, your minds have melded," I said.

"Thank you for that," said Dad. "May we ask how your semester went?"

I skirted the question. "Judge Chun is deciding what Peter Liang's sentence will be, so we're doing regular vigils outside the courthouse. The pro-Liang Chinese are there, too. Their numbers aren't like they were, but they still show up at the courthouse."

"I saw it in the papers," said Mom. "They had how many thousands marching? And you guys get a few dozen? Sounds to me like you were out-organized."

I thought about our counterprotest in Cadman Plaza against the pro-Liang Chinese, watching them pour in by the tens of thousands, with their signs of ONE TRAGEDY TWO VICTIMS and LIANG WAS A SCAPEGOAT and even images of Dr. King alongside one of his quotations on justice.

I wondered where these people had been all this time, at any of the dozens of rallies for people killed by the police. It was worse than if they'd been protesting something stupid, like the lack of Asians in Hollywood. This was an active betrayal. They were ruining all the post-'68 coalition building between Blacks and Asians, proclaiming that they didn't want solidarity, they didn't want to be people of color—they wanted to watch out for their own.

We watched the speakers take the stage, middle-aged Chinese men in boxy suits and women in floral-print scarves, who, judging by their jittery eagerness, their hard grips on the microphone, had never been to, let alone spoken before, a rally. But now they felt the power of protest, the rush of standing before a crowd that not only agreed with their private, whispered opinions, but shouted them aloud, affirmed their fledgling voices and naive politics.

And so the few dozen of us counterprotesters began to sing that movement anthem at the top of our voices: *Which side are you on, my people?* The haunting melody that floated up and then, in the second line, fell in a mirror image of itself—*Which side are you on*—as if the brutality of the situation took away the question mark, gave you one line to make up your mind, so that by the second it was a demand.

"That's not *organizing*," I said. "That's being racist."

"Who says they're mutually exclusive?" said Dad. "You know, these right-wing crazies, the Obama birthers and the Evangelicals—I hate to say it, but they're very organized."

"Organizing is about resisting power, not upholding it," I said.

"Who taught you that?" asked Mom. "Your friend who gave you the ugly haircut?"

I bit my lip.

"What I don't get," said Mom, "is why you want this kid to go to jail. You didn't do that for those white cops."

"It didn't come up," I said flatly. "None of them were indicted."

"Exactly!" said Mom. "The courts are trying to railroad this Asian boy."

"He *killed a man,* Mom," I said, ready for the argument. "If we're asking for Liang to be let off, we're essentially asking for white privilege, the right to kill Black folks without consequence."

Dad cleared his throat. "And your classes?" he asked.

The wavy-banged waiter returned with a tray and began dealing out little white plates of panchan. Another waiter appeared with a platter piled high with meat, red and marbled with fat, shining under the bright lights.

The waiter flipped thin slices of meat onto the grill, where they sizzled, sending up curls of smoke that fled into the metal mouth of the ventilation hood. He opened a palm to tell us that the meat was ready. Mom swung into action, placing a slice on my plate first, a cease-fire to the conversation.

I took a bite. The meat was earthy, fatty, and had just a touch of smoky, charcoal sear; it melted away after a couple of bites. I reached for another.

"It makes me happy to see my son eat," said Mom.

"So good," I said, mouth full. "The Korean food in New York is miserable."

"Why can't those Koreans get it together?"

"Because they don't have to. We're all desperate enough that we'll overpay for watery naengmyun on Thirty-Second Street."

Mom's motions took on urgency as she tossed another slice onto my plate. The meal swung into its chaotic rhythm: waiters swooped by to clear old plates then laid the great slabs of marinated beef and pork on the flames; steaming black earthenware bowls appeared, holding bubbling kimchi and doenjang stews. The K-pop blasting overhead gave it all a bouncy tempo.

Mom sat in the middle of it all like some jaded conductor, directing waiters to refill glasses and panchan, doling out the meat—always double portions for me—and moving bowls around with insistent, primal grunts of *try this* and *have some* so that flavors appeared in my mouth almost without my conscious input. But there they were, exploding with garlic and char and the bright red spice. Somehow, in all of this, Mom managed to feed herself, but in my frenzy of wrapping kalbi in lettuce and slurping broths, I didn't see her do it.

When it was over, all that remained was a blackened grill littered by bits of charred fat and a sea of small plates with pools of oil and soup in them. My stomach pressed against the waistline of my jeans and I leaned back to ease the pressure. A busboy came with a metal wand that he jammed into the grill and lifted it away, disappearing into the back so it could be scrubbed and offered to the next customer with a fresh, gleaming surface. He came back with a gray plastic tub and threw our plates into it with an unceremonious clatter.

"Isn't it messed up," I said, watching the busboy hurry away, "how all the waiters are Korean and all the busboys are Latino? That's a pretty clear example of racial capitalism, except we're supposed to feel okay because the owners are Korean instead of white."

"Gah, can we go for fifteen minutes without an ideological critique?" asked Mom.

"I just think we have to be aware of each interaction, or else we're blindly upholding the white supremacist heteropatriarchy."

"That's a mouthful," said Dad.

"How else would you say it?"

"Back then," said Mom, "we said, 'The Man.'"

I smiled, imagining a day when the kids would make fun of our generation for saying *intergenerational trauma* and *intersectionality*.

"I see they're teaching you something at Columbia," said Dad.

"Actually," I said, "I learned about racial capitalism through Twitter and meetings, not Columbia. Everything in college is designed to insulate us from the world, so we can patch over the neoliberal order without challenging anything structural."

"This is the son who cried when his acceptance letter came?" asked Mom.

"So I was drinking the ideological Kool-Aid of the private university," I said, blushing. "Everything pointed me that way: CJ got into Harvard, our teachers were throwing us parties. But once I actually got to Columbia, I met these privileged dummies from Connecticut who were only there because their grandparents had buildings named after them. It's a machine designed to perpetuate inequity."

Dad harrumphed. "Sorry to break this to you," he said, "but we could've told you that. Of course these neoliberal institutions want to perpetuate themselves. You're going to have to deal with them sooner or later, and now you have the privilege to learn how."

"Yes, yes, my privilege. Want to remind me how much tuition is, too?"

Dad flinched like I'd stuck him with a needle. "Grandma and Grandpa wanted you to have the best education possible."

"So I could participate in the great American ladder climb, where East Asians hoard resources and try to become white at the expense of Black and Brown people."

"Who the hell taught our son to talk this way?" Mom folded her arms and seemed to grow more solid in her seat. "I guess that's the point of these liberal colleges: learn to talk shit about your bourgeois parents."

My cheeks burned like someone was pressing the grill against them.

"That's right." Mom's eyes brightened with self-satisfaction. "Nothing new about it. Your father went through the whole denouncement thing, too. Luckily, your mother grew up poor in the third world. Tell them *that* next time to earn some 'good revolutionary' points."

Dad reddened, looking a little grilled himself. Mom had traced the line that always hovered invisibly between us, forming two lopsided is- lands within our little family. Mom was the immigrant from the back- water country most Americans knew, if they knew anything about it, as the normal half we saved from the pudgy-faced dictator.

Dad and I, on the other hand, had our comfortable upbringings, our shared references within Americana. His dad had lived the Chinese American dream: he had convinced his fellow immigrants to pay a lit- tle money now to his insurance company so the white devils wouldn't rob them of everything when they faced disaster or died. It was where the moneyed of Chinatown indemnified their jade and gold collections, their grocery stores, and—the asset with a near-sacred place in their immigrant hearts—their homes. It didn't make the family white-people rich, but it made them Chinatown rich, which meant the first thing they did was move out of Chinatown. And so began the long inter- generational climb that brought me to the Ivy League, something Dad's parents would've loved. Now I felt like a tourist traveling somewhere old and grand I'd dreamed about from photos, only to find it smelled like sewage.

The blood in my ears amplified the roar of the restaurant—the music bumping, grills hissing, plates tap-tapping against tables. "I'm on academic probation," I said, almost in a shout, as if to drown out the noise.

Mom and Dad froze as if they were animatronic and someone had cut the electricity.

"You were getting straight As," Dad insisted, as if I'd mispoken.

"Yeah, well. I'm not exactly going to classes. I can look up the readings on JSTOR and write better papers than these legacy kids. But whatever. I'm not interested in sitting around at some oak table debating well-meaning liberals on whether the police should be able to murder people in the street because of their skin color." My throat clamped, forcing the words out thin but loud. "We're going to find out any day if one of them is going to jail for it. This is a turning point, and I want to actually get out there, be part of direct actions, part of this *movement*." I paused to let the alarm spread across my parents' faces. "They can keep me on probation. I'm not going back next semester."

The two of them stared blankly, like I'd started speaking in another language.

III

"WHAT UP, FOOL!" CJ YELLED AS she ran toward the car. I smiled and reached over to open the passenger door of the Prius, which I'd borrowed to escape dinner. I'd parked in the lot underneath CJ's apartment building, a K-Town monolith with the address in oversized green letters on a white stucco wall. I'd never seen the inside, all my years knowing CJ, because, she'd told me, *Umma would slice your balls off. No men allowed.*

CJ climbed inside and slammed the car door shut. She wrapped me in one of her quick, strong hugs, like she was trying to pop a balloon.

"Sorry I'm late," she said. The zippers on her black jacket rattled as she did one of her impromptu dances, her arms shooting around in excitement. "I had to take this huge shit. No joke, it was that big." She held her index finger halfway down her forearm. "I had to break it up with the plunger."

I laughed at seeing CJ back to her old self, then realized what she was saying and mimed a retch.

She beamed her big, toothy smile and slapped my arm. "Where do you want to go?"

"The spot?"

"Perfect," she said. "I'm gonna roll this joint."

CJ balanced a little kit in her lap: rolling papers and ends, a baggie of weed, a red Bic lighter. She snipped the bud with the tips of her nails and placed the small, sticky grains in the thin paper chute with the seriousness of a watchmaker.

We both thought CJ had made it when she got into *Hah-bah-du*, guaranteeing, at worst, a lifetime job of tutoring for a hundred bucks an hour—thought she could finally drop the stress that choked her with every test, every big paper during high school. But the release never came. The grind of getting into Harvard only gave way to staying afloat there: navigating the students who treated Harvard like one more playground guaranteed since birth, the secret societies they formed to hold the line between themselves and the Dorm Crew workers like CJ who got there early to scrub toilets, the professors who condescended to or hit on her or both.

Finally, last semester, she sent me some texts about feeling dead and I took the Peter Pan bus up to see her. She didn't want to leave her dorm room, so the two of us sat on the blue carpet all weekend, smoking and watching season after season of *The Office* on her laptop. I only left to buy us shitty sandwiches from the Au Bon Pain in the square, two of them each time, though I knew she'd only nibble at hers and leave the rest in the minifridge.

I drove north, where the homes of millionaires glittered against the black mountains.

"Dude," she said. "How's your halmoni?"

I shook my head. "She looks terrible. Like, a different person."

"That fucking sucks."

"It's whatever," I said. "How are *you*?"

"Better, dude. Way better," she said forcefully. "I just needed to be away from all the fucking stress and cold for a minute."

"With the meds should you be—you know?" I looked at her rolling. CJ huffed. "Please. The meds plus a little weed and I'm floating."

"So you're going back?"

"Hell yeah. I'm gonna beat those dumb fuckers. Not because I need to prove shit, but because I freaking can, you know? I actually need to start planning my thesis for next year," she said, an excited buzz coming into her voice. "I'm thinking about Joyce."

"Seriously?" I blurted. "I'm so done with the 'core' curriculum. What are you going to learn from some dead white man going on about his amazing thoughts as he walks around?"

"Ew," she said. "Don't come at me with that Twitter social justice shit." She slapped my arm again. "Have you even read *Ulysses*?"

"Do I need to read it to know it reifies a Eurocentric, patriarchal world view?"

She sighed as if she felt sorry for me. "Remember how I used to joke that the Irish were the Koreans of Europe? They're alcoholics, always fighting and beating their wives, because they're stuck in a broke, tiny-ass country that was colonized? Anyway, I read *Ulysses* and I was like, *I get this shit*. It's about how history fucks with the psyche, and constituting a postcolonial selfhood." CJ waited for a response from me, and seeing none, chopped her hand against her pelvis. "Suck it."

I chuckled out of embarrassment. The "core" had become my nemesis, a two-year slog through dozens of dead white men until we got a brief breath of Toni Morrison or Frantz Fanon at the end. Ash was a year older and told me not to wait that long: I skimmed Plato and Rousseau to get to the Audre Lorde and the Combahee River Collective she handed me. But judging from the grades I was getting back, it was showing.

Maybe, though, I'd turned that fight into a sort of laziness. I was used to saying something damning about the great white canon and everyone else in the room nodding, whether or not I or they had read it. CJ never cared about that—she tore through everything with equal force, able to read her life in the lives of others.

CJ sniffed the air, brought her nose to her armpit, and then let out a bleating noise. "Can I tell you something? This shirt smells like BO. I was like, why? I don't smell like that." She tugged at the shirt, a thin black fabric studded with silver beads. "I realized it's from some white girl who tried it on before me at the store. I smell like some fucking white girl's BO now. I want to *die*."

I laughed so hard I had to steady the wheel.

"Stop laughing!" she said, laughing too. "Fuck it, I'm going to take it off and just wear my jacket." She undid her seat belt and squirmed out of her jacket, then pulled the shirt off over her head and stuffed it into her purse.

My eyes darted toward her body, then away. The way she undressed had always been a relief, all those long afternoons in high school when we were sort of dating. It had no tease, no self-consciousness to it. She understood the baroque gender constructs of high school sexuality—she always had the best slim jeans, taught others how to apply eyeliner—but carried herself like a tomboy. I never understood the rules of that game, and it was a relief to be with someone who didn't need me to play it.

She zipped her jacket up to the top. "Maybe it's different in New York, but East Coast bitches are so basic, it's like, why even bother dressing well?"

"Only if you go downtown. The white kids on campus all wear the same North Face fleece."

"Ugh," she turned to me. "Let's make a pact never to wear that shit."

"Would sooner get hypothermia."

We slid palms and bumped fists. It was a gesture I didn't know was particular to L.A. until the first day of college when I held my palm out to someone who cocked his head, then shook it, stiffly, as if I were a trained animal.

"Anyway, I won't be around those kids anymore," I said. "I'm dropping out."

"For real?" CJ's eyes widened. "That's fucking crazy. What did your parents say?"

"They went into shock."

"Dude," she said slowly. "My momma said she would stab me, then stab herself, so she could haunt me forever as a ghost if I didn't go back next semester. Be glad your mom's so chill."

"Wow," I said, appreciating her imagination. "I wouldn't exactly call my mom 'chill.'"

"What are you going to do instead?"

"Organize. March. Work outside the bubble."

"Ohh!" exclaimed CJ. "It's because of your intense-ass Columbia friends. The ones who are all, *Burn the system down.*"

I'd introduced CJ to Tiff and Ash when she visited me in New York, thinking they'd get along because of their shared don't-fuck-with-me sureness. But the combination backfired: CJ started mocking the middle-class kids at Harvard organizing with the striking cafeteria workers, until it turned out Tiff and Ash were friends with them through labor groups. I sat there listening for a tense half hour, all of us sitting in the uncomfortable blond wood chairs of my dorm room, until finally CJ offered to light a joint. The one thing they all had in common was that and a love for Erykah Badu, whose raspy voice emanated from my MacBook, as we relaxed onto the floor in a tense silence.

"It was my idea," I shot back. "I mean, as a middle-class East Asian kid, I feel like it's really the only option; otherwise, the degree is just another resource I'm hoarding, propelling myself up the ladder toward whiteness."

Silence fell and I was listening, I realized, for a sign of CJ's approval.

"*Pffft.*" She cackled. "Damn, you need to destress and smoke some good-ass Cali weed." She held up the joint, thin and elegant, tapered smoothly to a point where a little tab of cardboard served as the mouthpiece.

"Still the master," I said.

"Mastery is a Western patriarchal construct," CJ said in a heavy voice mocking mine, then she slapped my arm and we laughed.

We crossed Sunset Boulevard into Laurel Canyon. The mountains rose on either side as the street narrowed and the light and noise of the city dropped away. I'd missed this drive, the calm and focus it demanded, a quiet tunnel through the city.

We came to the mountaintop and I turned onto Mulholland Drive—named after the white man who'd stolen water for L.A. I'd learned in my ethnic studies class how this city was taken from Mexico and advertised as a white haven away from the grimy East—a lie that Hollywood exploded around the world. But the whites were upset to arrive and find it was already Brown, would soon be Black and Yellow, and so retreated into the hills where they could live on streets called Mulholland and gaze down at the smoggy, colored basin below.

The road grew darker and windier. There was no reason to come here unless you were visiting one of the mansions, or doing exactly what we were doing. I parked in the small lot with a sign warning in bold letters that it closed at sunset. We stepped onto the gravel and leaned against the hood in the darkness. The engine was still warm, clicking and hissing. The city spread below us, a field of orange streetlamps and red and white car lights in an endless grid to the very edge of the horizon. A band of muddy air hovered above it, gathering the light.

"Not bad," I said.

"Yeah," said CJ. "What the fuck did we know? Turns out the East Coast sucks, and most of the shit I wanted to get away from was me."

CJ lit the joint and the tip burst into red curls as she inhaled, a flash of light amid the darkness of the mountaintop. She handed me the joint then let the smoke seep from her mouth.

"Be careful with this shit."

I puffed. The vapor moved down my throat like scalding soup. I coughed and handed it back. It left a taste of berries and ash. Dullness bloomed through my brain and I looked down at my hands to make sure they were still there. "I think I'm good."

"Lightweight," CJ chuckled and puffed away.

"When we were visiting Halmoni," I said, slowly, feeling my tongue loll around my mouth, "I tried to ask my mom about her past. She wouldn't talk about it, but that doesn't stop her guilt-tripping me for my bad life choices."

"Duh," CJ fluttered her lips. "You're Korean."

"Half. What does that have to do with it?"

"Just two centuries of colonialism and war and poverty."

I reached for the joint, sensing we were going somewhere I didn't want to go and needing to dull the feeling.

"I'm Asian *American*, though," I said. "Half of our work with the Liang-Gurley trial is to show we're not all Asians focused on their small businesses, totally ignorant of the racial context that allows them to succeed."

"Good luck with that," CJ said coldly.

I winced as I realized CJ's mom was one of those people. She'd run a dry cleaner on the edge of K-Town for years, where the clientele was mostly Latino. CJ would prop her AP calculus textbook against the register during her shifts. She'd tell me about the small dramas: the man who always stumbled in drunk and hit on her mom, the constant little repairs for machinery and lights that ate at their profits, the white people who screamed at them about little stains on their clothes. I'd always nodded as if I understood, but both of us knew I didn't.

"I mean, not like they're doing something wrong," I said, "just that our project is about the American context."

CJ flicked the last of the joint away and grunted. "You remember in high school, when my mom was in the hospital?"

I nodded.

CJ shifted in her jacket and her silhouette grew hard. "When she was lying there recovering, she started to tell me all this shit about her life, how she was depressed because of being lonely in this country where she didn't know anyone and didn't have time for anything but the fucking dry cleaner. How sometimes she wanted to vanish.

"And then I left to go back to school. She got better and went right back to working so she wouldn't have to think about how depressed she was. Some *Candide* shit. Anyway, I got it, then: of course she was such a dick to me all the time, of course everything in my life—studying, Harvard, all that—was for her, even though I didn't know it. Her depression, her wishing it was all different, was soaked into me before I was *born*. But if she never told me that stuff in the hospital, I'd just think she was some crazy bitch who happened to be my mom."

CJ hunched forward and shoved her hands into her pockets. "Of course your mom's not going to make it easy. But you have to figure that inherited shit out before it fucks you up worse. Freaking Korean moms."

"Yeah," I muttered. *Korean moms.* It felt like CJ had brought us to some totem inscribed in symbols we could sound out phonetically but didn't understand. Whatever it meant, it wasn't the all-American tenderness that bonded mother and child.

"Blah!" CJ yelled. She stuck her tongue out and threw her arms in the air as if she were drowning and signaling a ship. "Blerrr! Next topic! I'm tired of being all fucking serious. Let's get boba or something."

IV

MOM CAUGHT ME SHUFFLING TO-ward the coffee machine. "Out with CJ all night, smoking that Mary Jane?" she exclaimed, an inspector solving a too-easy case.

I looked at the dull green lines of the stove clock and saw it was past ten, which meant one in the afternoon, New York time. I sniffed my shirt but didn't detect any trace of weed. "'Mary Jane'?" I deflected. "Come on, Mom."

"Uh-*huh*. Mothers know some things." She swung her arms in wide arcs from side to side, slapping her shoulders and kidneys with loud thwacks, some ancient Daoist morning routine she'd recently begun. "No wonder your grades are slipping."

I rubbed my eyes and inserted a capsule into the machine, one of those sleek, pod-based towers that added to the plastic gyre in the ocean with each serving. I pushed a button and the inside roared, sending a creamy string of espresso into my cup. I took a sip and the liquid was eerily rich and fresh, coming from that vacuum-sealed pod. More importantly, my nervous system tingled to life.

"Smoking is just a form of self-medicating to deal with the anxieties of late capitalism," I said. "It's one of the least self-destructive things I can imagine."

"*Please*. Do what you want. I went to college, too, you know—the stuff always just made me sleepy."

I added this to the sketchy picture I had of Mom's Berkeley years. "Thank you for that. I'll carry forward the family tradition of fighting the Man and smoking Mary Jane."

Mom wagged her hand at me. "I never said you *should* do it. You slept till ten and still you look like hell." She pulled down the flesh under her eyes to illustrate. "I'm saying you should learn from your mother's mistakes."

She stopped swinging her arms and gestured toward the dining room table. I sat across from her and ran my hands over the dark grain of the wooden top. It was a new addition. A trapezoid of morning light fell across it and caught the steam rising from my coffee cup. The whole thing was ready to Instagram, a perfect image of the bourgie comforts Mom had cultivated piece by piece to create catalog-ready images like this.

Mom folded her hands on the table. "I don't support this dropping-out plan, and not just because I'm your mother. I've been there and it's painful, the whole Black-Asian situation." She inhaled as if about to dive underwater. "Your mother cofounded something called the Black-Korean Coalition in the 1980s, to stop all the violence in South Central."

My mind lit up, blazing a connection between Mom's words and the half dozen meetings and teach-ins on Black-Asian solidarity we'd held in the last year, trying to string together an alternative history, proving that we were more than shopkeepers harassing their Black customers, parents suing to overturn affirmative action.

But the histories had started to feel thin. I thought of all the pictures I'd seen of Yuri Kochiyama—a Nissei grandma with her permed hair but wearing a FREE MUMIA T-shirt—and Grace Lee Boggs—the revolutionary theorist who organized urban farms in Detroit. I'd heard so many spoken word tributes, had watched so many indie documentaries on them that—though I'd never say so out loud—the attachment was starting to feel a little desperate. They were exceptions proving the rule of Asian anti-Blackness, lighthouses accentuating the fogginess of the coastline.

"Mom," I said. "Wow. We need that story. This had to be related to Rodney King and the L.A. uprising, right? Sa-i-gu?" 4-2-9, the abbreviated Korean name for the April day their stores were set aflame, a low point in our Black-Asian timeline. "This would totally remake the popular narrative. Maybe you could lead a workshop or teach-in for us. Or we could do an oral history?"

"Wah, I've never seen my son so eager to talk to me," she gasped sarcastically. "It's not exactly a happy story."

"No, of course. I mean, we'd have to take a trauma-informed approach—"

"My son." She put up a palm to stop me. "There are things I'm happy to share if they help you understand what you're doing out there. But I'm not going to polish it into some tool kit you can circulate to your activist friends. These young organizers always come to me saying, *Ahh, Aunty, can you mentor me?* And I say to them, *First, I'm not your aunty—I'm not that old. And second, what the fuck for? I don't have any answers.* Usually they just want someone to listen to their problems."

I pictured all of my activist friends saying exactly that, the yearning and eagerness in their faces. And I felt my own desperation, my sudden childlike need. "Exactly—it shows how few Asian American activist models we have. Most of my friends' parents and grandparents don't even support Black Lives Matter, let alone teach them movement history."

"'Movement history'? Gah, you make me sound old!" Mom crossed her arms, smug at having the upper hand. "Aren't you grateful to have such a cool mother?"

"Yes, yes," I muttered.

"Just thinking about it makes me tense." She hiked her shoulders up and rocked her neck between them. "Let's go to yoga to loosen up, then I'll tell you more."

"I sense a deal being struck."

Mom grinned. "Where'd you learn to be so sharp?"

* * *

We drove through Brentwood toward the yoga studio, passing storefronts filled with BMWs, "oriental" rugs, and designers I'd never heard of. Every building gleamed white, a Mediterranean fantasy that left no trace of the workers who polished those facades.

I took out my phone to text Tiff.

Listen

I found a Black-Asian solidarity story—from guess where?

My mom

I'm kinda jealous of your family
we def need that story
maybe you could write a blog post for us

I smiled to myself. Until that point I'd been a naive, privileged kid trying to build my analytical parachute mid–free fall. Here was something I could finally offer to the movement.

I'd never live down my first encounter with Tiff after our Chinatown meal. They stood on the quad wearing a Band-Aid on their left cheek and tried to slow the students passing by. They remembered my name, as a good organizer does, and called out to me so I couldn't duck away like the other students. Tiff spoke urgently about how a Black student had been crossing campus late at night, when a campus cop asked him for his ID. They got into an argument and the cop "accidentally" pushed the student to the ground. The student scraped his knee, hence the Band-Aid.

"So," they said, handing me one, "it would be great if you wore this, in solidarity."

I took the tiny paper wrapper, mumbled a thanks, avoided their sharp, eyelinered gaze, and turned away. I walked out the campus gates and tossed it into one of the big, green trash cans on Amsterdam Avenue, afraid that someone would see me and that it would somehow get back to Tiff. The Band-Aid struck me as some pointless, embarrassing performance. Plus, I thought, if the student had just shown his ID he could've avoided the whole interaction.

This was after Trayvon, yes, but before Renisha McBride, before Michael Brown and Tamir Rice and Eric Garner, before Freddie Gray, before Akai Gurley. Before it had dawned on me, and millions of other half-woke liberals, that this was no coincidence, no occasional hiccup, but part of the design of the country. The new knowledge made me nauseous as I remembered the Band-Aid and all the thousands of times I'd written off police violence as exaggerated or innocent mistakes. And so when Gurley's case went to trial, and Tiff and Ash offered a workshop on cross-racial solidarity, I showed up. Tiff went up to me after the meeting and soon I was cochairing a committee on student outreach; I was the one on the steps handing out the flyers.

Mom glanced over as we idled at a red light. "Texting with those friends of yours—what's-her-name who gave you the bad haircut?"

I felt defensive, as if they were in the next room. "Tiff goes by *they* pronouns, Mom."

Mom blinked. "I don't get all this stuff. In Korean, we don't have pronouns."

"Okay," I said. I took a breath and stopped myself from flipping out and accusing Mom of heteronormativity. I had, after all, only learned this myself a couple years before. "Your generation made a big deal about not being called 'orientals,' right? And now we're Asian Americans, which at least doesn't sound like that carpet store we just passed. Our generation feels like gender is a social construct, not a biological fact, and so we need pronouns to reflect that."

Mom blinked. "Uh-huh. So she says 'they'?"

"*They* say 'they.'"

"Ach," Mom rasped. "How is she—I mean he, they, whatever?"

"Mom. 'Whatever'?"

She gripped the steering wheel so hard it squeaked. "Okay, I'll try harder. In return, maybe you can be a little softer on your old mother? It's very hard when all of a sudden young people make up a new gender."

It seemed as much of a victory as I was going to get in the moment. "Thank you," I said flatly, as I held back saying that the only ones making anything up were cis people and their two rigid categories. Assuming I got Mom to open up about her past and offer a model of Black-Asian solidarity work, then convince her why I needed to quit school and dedicate myself to the movement, we'd need a whole reckoning around gender and sexuality. Meanwhile the world was on fire and it would take all we had to face this one case of police violence and the conservative Asians backing it.

"Ai," Mom rasped. "Stop slouching."

* * *

"Oh my gosh." The woman behind the counter—white, of course, and wearing a tank top of futuristic rubber that somehow glinted both purple and orange—swiveled her neck from Mom to me with a fixed smile as she reached for Mom's credit card. "Mother and son? *That's* adorable."

Mom beamed and patted me on the head. "I've got to teach this one some self-care."

"Yah," she exhaled knowingly. She placed a form in front of me and drew a loopy *X* where I needed to sign away my right to sue if I slipped a disc while backbending. "And your mom's paying? Ugh," she said, so envious she was disgusted.

A door swung open behind the desk and a woman with a ponytail and headset burst out. The room beyond was dark, and a bluish glow seeped from the ceiling. Drake's grainy voice boomed inside and the beat sent vibrations through my chest. The ponytailed woman skipped across the lobby giving high fives.

Mom waved at the woman. "Hey, Ari!"

"Hey, girlie!" Ari rushed toward us. She reached for a high five and her muscles rippled like a cheetah's. Her palm crashed into mine, rattling the bones in my elbow joint. "Your mom. Slays. I cannot believe she's, I mean, I don't even know how old? But this class is no joke."

"Wow. She didn't tell me that."

"Don't worry, you're young. And you can *always* do child's pose."

"Is that like, sitting on the floor cross-legged?" But Ari had already turned to hug the woman behind us. I followed Mom into the dark, Drake-filled room and unfurled a rubber mat next to her. She lay on her back and brought her legs into her chest, limber for someone I-don't-even-know-how-old. A stream of statuesque white people flowed into the room, emitting odors of shea butter and sage oil, and began lifting their legs at impossible angles.

The door closed and we were cast into darkness, outlined in blue light, like some sexy commercial for a Vegas club. The beat whomped through the room and the chatter died down, replaced by Ari's voice booming through the sound system.

"All right, 11:30! I just want to know—did you come here to do *stretches?*" she said in a schoolyard whine. "Or did you come to *work*? I *said!* Did you come here to *work*?" People in the room whooped. Someone did a celebratory handstand. "Okay! Come into downward dog."

I looked around at people's inverted triangles and pushed myself up to mimic them. My palms were disconcertingly slick against the mat. I wiped each hand against the opposite sleeve, and as I shifted, a little drop of sweat fell from my forehead.

"Is it hot?" I whispered to Mom.

"Oh yeah, that's the best part. She keeps it like that to loosen your muscles."

It was as if someone had designed a special hell for me: a darkened furnace pumped with mass-market hip-hop and filled with preening white Hollywooders.

Ari yelled at us to jump up to the front of our mats. The woman next to me sprang in slow motion: her bottom half floated upward and arced forward slowly, insulting gravity and landing without a sound just behind her wrists. I gaped and then clambered forward on my mat, having just signed away my right to sue if I broke something.

The drip of sweat became a generous beading. I felt it pool at the base of my back. Mom was sweating, too—everyone was—but they all ignored it so that instead of being something gross it became a hard-earned glow. That was why people did yoga: exertion to simulate actual *work* without any of the self-examination of, say, understanding white supremacy.

I looked up and the glamorous yoga robots were all staring at me. I was facing the wrong way. The darkness hid my blushing and I paid closer attention to Ari's dyslexia-inducing instructions—right leg back, right arm under left thigh, left arm across—and reversed my stance. Calf muscles I'd never felt quietly tore apart. The woman next to me reached under her thigh to wrap around and meet her other hand, making a human pretzel. Her neck swiveled up with swanlike grace. I glared with hatred.

The beads of sweat started to sluice down as if I were in a scummy shower. But everyone moved steadily from one pose to the next as if they'd all rehearsed this slow dance together. I felt the peer pressure forcing me to continue, my body now a puppet for the wellness gurus monetizing this ancient practice and shaping me in their own image.

Ari appeared by my side and covered her headset with one hand. "Don't worry," she said, her white teeth gleaming insincerely in the blue light, "just take child's pose."

"What the *fuck* is—" I started, but she'd stepped beside the swanlike woman and caressed her shoulders so that they stood half an inch more level, like a sculptor buffing a nearly finished marble.

I dragged my body from pose to pose. Mom was able to keep up with the yoga divas, and in spite of everything I was impressed.

"All right! I think we've earned a cooldown," said Ari.

Tears of relief slid from my eyes, dewy and embarrassing. Ari directed us onto our backs, and as I lay down I felt like the floor was alive and cradling my sore body.

"Now for the hardest pose of all," said Ari, her voice now lilting and New Agey. "Corpse pose." She told us how to splay our limbs and pull our shoulder blades beneath us. "Why is it hard?" She'd cut out the music, and her elongated vowels wafted through the room. "Because we want to keep moving, want to keep distracting ourselves, and this pose asks us to simply surrender. To just. Give. Up."

I stared at the ceiling and plotted my revenge against Mom for tricking me into coming here. No cross-generational lesson was worth this torture. I'd post on Twitter about the new lows of cultural appropriation being peddled in L.A. and hopefully amass a minor swarm of others to mock the studio, shame them into an apology.

"If you feel your mind drifting around," Ari chimed, "offer it the gift of just being here, now."

I closed my eyes. There wasn't anything here, now, except the sweat crystalizing on my skin and clumping my hair.

I felt a hand slapping my thigh. I opened my eyes to Mom crouching over me. The lights were on and the room had emptied out. A couple stragglers were rubbing each other's shoulders affectionately and I couldn't tell if they were lovers, or friends, or had just met and appreciated each other's energies.

"Sleeping Beauty up?" Mom chuckled. "Must've been a good workout."

Ari crouched at my other side. She gave Mom a fist bump then looked down at me. "You did awesome. I mean, your mom kills. But for your first class?"

I sat up and felt, with great surprise and resentment, that part of me wanted Ari's approval. "Thanks," I said.

"Maybe one day you'll catch up to me," said Mom. "Hah!" She flexed a bicep and pointed with her other hand.

"Your mom is hilarious. And next time you can always—"

"Totally." I stood up and accepted another fracturing high five.

I followed Mom out of the studio. "There will never be a next time," I said. I blinked against the bright sun, astonished that it had been there the whole time, right outside that dark, sweaty box.

"So dramatic, Reed!" she said. "Don't you feel good?"

"I feel like I've been turned into mush."

"Isn't that the best?" Mom took a deep breath and rolled her shoulders back.

I paid attention to my body as we crossed the parking lot toward the car. My head was buoyant on my neck, a balloon pulling the rest of me a little bit straighter, and the ground was soft, as if the asphalt had turned to warm rubber. I noticed the gentle pulsing of my blood from my heart to my fingertips.

"Aha!" said Mom. "You feel it, don't you? Just imagine if you went once a week."

"Instead of fighting for racial justice I could just get little endorphin rushes for twenty bucks a pop."

"Who said you had to choose?"

"How can these things coexist?" I raised my voice. "How was it an overheated coffin in there, and the usual bright desert out here? How can people be marching against police violence in Brooklyn right now, as we were doing baby poses? I can't deal with the contradiction."

Mom huffed. She thumbed her key and the car chirped. "You'd better learn to deal."

I slid into the car and flopped onto the seat. "Okay, bringing it back to you—which was the other half of this deal—when you were an activist, you weren't doing yoga."

"No," said Mom, going through the automatic L.A. motions of buckling up as she backed the car out. "But it would've been a hell of a lot smarter if we were."

"Let's address the racialized exploitation between Asians and Blacks by having them do yoga together."

"You talk, my smartass son, but things like that are how you actually connect people. That's lesson one for your little tool kit."

I paused. "Go on," I said, hesitant but curious.

"Organizing is person-to-person, right? And do most people like to sit around in meetings talking about blah-blah *racial capitalism*? Or do fun things, like sharing food, or exercising, or listening to music?"

I hadn't used the word *fun* in a while. I thought back to the karaoke night Tiff had invited me to with some organizers in Chinatown. We sat around the red vinyl booths at Winnie's drinking Millers and flipping through fat binders to match a song to a number that the salty bartender would queue into the machine for a dollar. The night gathered momentum as we drank and egged each other on, and I was dumbfounded to see everyone singing the same campy power ballads and early 2000s R&B songs you'd hear at any millennial karaoke. I suppose I'd expected more Talib Kweli, if not, say, "The Internationale." But watching people throw themselves at the mic—these organizers who intimidated me with their analyses and sharp retorts—bellowing with abandon, tearing up at the chorus, then smiling pure joy as they bowed to our roars of admiration, I understood that we all needed a release.

That was only a few months ago, but the trial had escalated and we'd gotten steadily busier, and it seemed impossible to feel that carefree again. I felt tired. "Well," I snapped, "there's nothing *fun* about this moment, when innocent people are dying."

Mom sighed. "When is it ever? Not South Central in the eighties, I promise." She swiped on her turn signal to change course. "I can't argue with you. I have to show you."

V

MOM SLOWED THE CAR OUTSIDE A building with a low, trapezoidal roof and mirrored windows, the kind of building that was everywhere in L.A. but would never exist in New York: a sprawling, one-story that blocked the sun rather than soaking in every inch of it. L.A. had its temples to bourgie living, but the city was mostly these squat, functional boxes.

"You must be hungry," said Mom.

My stomach gurgled and I looked up at the sign, where a happy-looking rooster stood in front of a round, yellow grid. "Roscoe's Chicken and Waffles?" I chuckled. I hadn't been there for years, not since Mom had started her workout routines and diets. "Seems a little incongruous with the yoga."

"Normally I wouldn't," said Mom, getting out of the car. "But I'll make an exception for our little history lesson."

Inside, the low roof succeeded in keeping the sun out, and the dim room felt outside of time. Pink neon tubes lined the ceiling and gave everyone in the dark brown booths a rosy glow.

The host gestured to us and we slid into a booth. The plastic squeaked against our bare skin and exercise clothes. Mom scanned the laminated menu. Again, I didn't bother looking. A waiter with a crisp white polo shirt came by.

"Hey, how you doing?" said Mom.

The waiter nodded. "All right."

"We'd like chicken and waffles."

"That's what we do," he said affirmingly.

"Dark meat only."

"Uh-huh."

Mom asked about the biscuits, then the greens, then the different combination platters. The waiter's bemused smile grew with each question, while I sunk lower into the booth. Their back-and-forth suggested we were about to end up with another obscene amount of food.

"Nice to other waiters," I pointed out as he left.

"Ai. At Korean restaurants I'm too gruff, here I'm too nice. It's cultural, you know, when a young brother comes to the table, you talk."

I glanced around to see if anyone was listening. "I think you're using AAVE in a way that's not really appropriate?"

"Using what?"

"African American Vernacular English. You know, *how you doing, brother*."

"Is this one of your young-people things?"

"It's about a pattern of non-Black people saying *turn up* and *yaaas* and terms that, thanks to Twitter, are appropriated almost as soon as they originate. Or, even worse, white people yelling *I can't breathe* and *Whose streets? Our streets!* at protests, as if them falsely identifying with Black suffering and claiming ownership of public space weren't exactly the problem."

Mom looked at me blankly. "That's just how we talked back in the day. You know, *sister, brother*. It's a term of endearment."

"But is he? *Your* brother?"

Mom grunted. "If we can't be familiar with each other, how the hell are we going to organize together?"

"We have to recognize difference first."

She looked at me with something like concern. "You know, I was fresh off the boat when I went to Berkeley. I learned English in Oakland. People had never seen an ESL Korean woman saying *sister* and *the pigs* and *all power to the people*. It surprised them, but it also built trust and connection—which made me an effective organizer in this history you supposedly want to learn about."

I tried to imagine this time before social media, when you didn't have an online persona, only your actual persona; before you could pull some stranger's words from the great feed and invite thousands of others to drag them. And in that context, maybe solidarity meant sharing language and culture. Of course, I would never state Mom's case on Twitter myself, for fear of getting dragged.

"Okay, generational difference," I conceded, while also not wanting Mom to gloat. I asked why we were there, anyway.

"Do you remember Bobby?"

I nodded. Bobby was the thin Black man who'd come up to me every year in the middle of my parents' Christmas party, make eye contact through his wire-rim glasses, and say, *Your mom, man. Back in the day—whew!* Then he'd shake his head, laughing at this inside joke with himself, and walk away.

"We both worked for the county in the eighties," said Mom. "I was the community liaison for Koreatown and he was the head of South Central relations—L.A.'s racial politics were obvious like that. The two of us started talking right away because of all the violence. You know: Korean merchants arguing with Black customers, getting into fights, shooting. My people," Mom wagged her head.

"We'd be out in South Central all day," she continued, "and there was nowhere to eat except Roscoe's! We came here all the time and I loved it. So the point is you have to find ways to actually enjoy the work together, otherwise you burn out."

I glanced around the room and tried to square the kid at the next table licking his fingers with the old footage of people smashing windows. "But it's not like you actually accomplished any *organizing* here."

Mom mimed slapping me on the head. "So literal. You should know the relationships you build between organizers are part of the work."

I was silent as I considered that blurry line between friendship and organizing, and how I never really knew which was happening with Tiff and the others, and whether that was healthy or dangerous or both.

"Bobby was excited because I was the first Korean organizer he'd met," Mom continued. "He'd tried speaking to Korean merchants but, you know, the language and cultural barriers. I could translate and actually get stuff done. We started to convene these groups of Korean merchants and Black community leaders to speak face-to-face and called it the Black-Korean Coalition."

I smiled at this image of the two crisscrossing South Central like some racial justice investigative duo, the very sight of a Black man and Korean woman committed to racial healing shocking and heartening to people.

"That's pretty cool, Mom," I said. "I mean, that's radical for something that happened, like, thirty years ago."

Mom huffed. "You make it sound like some ancient history."

"No, it's just—we could barely find recent examples of Black-Asian solidarity, let alone before '92. It also seems politically significant that you were supporting Black businesses, if one of the main issues was how many were Korean owned."

"Oh, now my son is telling me what the issues were?"

"South Central was a food desert, right? We learned this in my ethnic studies class. And Korean merchants were opening up liquor stores when what people really needed was a grocery store."

Mom looked away and exhaled slowly, like a release valve on a pressure cooker. "First off, *professor*, most of them sold produce and dry goods, not just liquor. Second, it takes a lot of capital to open up a grocery store, which most Koreans didn't have. And," she said with triumph, "may I point out that you got this whole analysis from that college education you're eager to throw away?"

"Well—" I stammered. "Aren't you saying two things here? That my college education is useless, because it removes me from firsthand organizing experience, and I should stick with it anyway?"

"All I'm saying, my son, is to not take your precious theories so seriously."

The waiter walked toward us. He set down a tray and placed two huge, beige, plastic plates in front of each of us. One plate was piled with fried chicken, while the other held two oversized, fluffy waffles and two silver cups filled to the brim with maple syrup and a ball of butter, scooped like ice cream. Next to these, he placed a comically small bowl of greens.

I scraped the butter into the square craters of the waffles, then poured the syrup over the stack and took a bite. Then I sliced open the chicken thigh with a satisfying crackle and took a bite of that. The salty-sweet taste and the fluff of waffle against the crunch of chicken filled my mouth and I had nothing to say. Mom was immersed in her food, too, and I realized we'd both been hungry and edgy.

"Mmm!" exclaimed Mom. "Here," she placed an extra chicken thigh on my plate. "I'm going to have to hit that yoga class every day now. See what happens when you're in town?"

I looked down at my pyramid of breaded meat. "Uh, this was your idea."

"Was it? Well, you're welcome. Isn't it just delicious?" Mom smiled to show that the sin of eating chicken with waffles added to the pleasure of it.

I nodded, chewed, and considered Mom's living history, the unofficial meeting place of her solidarity work. "Did Bobby like to eat this much?"

"Oh sure," said Mom. "That's why we got along. He took me here, I took him to Korean barbecue. He loved kalbi."

"Okay, that's kind of cute," I said. "So if there was this potential for connection, why did the tension keep escalating?"

"There were many different pockets in the so-called Korean community. A lot of Korean grocers would say, *What issue? There's no issue. I like my Black customers, they like me.* They just thought if they stayed in denial and played nice, it would blow over."

"That's actually fascinating," I said. "You know, all the readings we do are centered around the Black struggle, around policing. But there's so little on Asians and policing, let alone an understanding of intra-community politics. And we're facing the same issue—a split inside the community."

"Exactly," Mom jabbed the air. "That's the biggest challenge—figuring out your own people."

I'd once tried to start a similar conversation with Tiff, and I saw anger flash across their face before they hid it with a smile. "What if now's not the time to center us, to take up space?" I said to Mom, repeating Tiff's answer to me.

"What space?" asked Mom.

I laughed. "Not, like, literal space. You know, inserting ourselves into a political dynamic when we should be supporting."

"What's the point of that?" Mom exclaimed. "You'd just be covering up the issues, or playing nice and serving up bullshit. It looks good in the beginning, but then it starts to stink."

I didn't disagree with Mom but didn't know how to place that against the possibility that organizing our side might be another subtle form of anti-Blackness, in which we were diverting attention from where it was needed. Perhaps both things were true, or it depended on context, or there was some third way that I wasn't seeing.

I chewed my waffles. The thought of presenting this at a teach-in made my head sore.

Mom nudged me and pointed at the extra thigh she'd given me, which sat untouched. "Eat up, so you don't freeze that skinny butt off marching!"

"You say I look skinny every time I come home."

"And you need a haircut. How about this?" she said, brightening. "Why don't we go to the Korean spa, so you can get scrubbed, then we go for a haircut?" Mom reached over and pinched the flap of my ear down, then nodded to herself like a doctor confirming the worst. "You'll feel like a new person."

I ducked away from her fingers. "A neoliberal idea if there ever was one."

"You should be thanking your mother! I swear, if I had a daughter she'd be begging me to do this stuff."

"I'm storing that one for future therapy sessions around Asian emasculation," I said. "How about *this*: I'll do that stuff, but I want to interview Bobby, hear his side of things."

Mom put down the hot sauce she'd been shaking over her chicken. She looked at me, as if gauging how serious I was. "Gah, who taught you to bargain like that?" She held her hand out to me, the fingers lustrous from chicken fat. "Deal."

VI

I PULLED UP TO BOBBY'S HOUSE IN Inglewood and saw that it was an odd mirror of my parents': the same Spanish style, when L.A. advertised itself to the country as a sunny ranch to escape the cold and gray of the old America. A plane flew overhead, splitting the air with its booming roar, then another. Of course LAX was plopped next to one of the few middle-class Black neighborhoods in the city.

I shut off the engine and felt the nerves along my neck tingle. Bobby, being retired, had agreed to meet me right when Mom called. I wasn't sure what to say to this person, whom I barely knew except for those ominous Christmas party run-ins. But no cross-racial organizing story would be complete if I didn't hear from him.

I rang the bell and a little dog began yapping. Bobby opened the door. His hair had grown whiter, his skin a little more papery, but otherwise his long face and goatee were just as I remembered.

"Reed, man, come on in," he said. We shook hands. He pointed to my feet. "Don't worry about the shoes. You probably don't remember this, but one time I went over to your house for a party, and everyone turned around and yelled, *Bobby! Shoes!*"

Some of my nervousness dropped away and I smiled at this image of him learning this custom second nature to all the East Asians I knew—a custom he remembered all these years.

The little dog leapt up and ran its paws against my leg. I'd never known how to interact with dogs. Mom once told me she'd eaten dogs, in Korea, when they were poor, and the closest I'd had to a pet was Dad letting me name the crabs he picked up in Chinatown before he boiled them alive. I never repeated any of this to non-Asians, knowing it would confirm our barbarism in their minds. I mimicked people on TV and let the dog sniff my hand.

Bobby told me not to mind Jeanette. He picked her up and gestured toward the big couches in the living room. The wooden slat blinds were closed, so the room was dark and cool, another instance of the L.A. aversion to sunlight. I collapsed onto the sofa. Bobby sat across from me as Jeanette sniffed around my ankles.

"Thanks so much for meeting with me," I said, putting a glossy red gift bag on the table. "From my mom."

Bobby peered into the bag and removed the box of cookies inside, some French assortment that Mom knew he'd like. Bobby wagged a finger at me. "Your mom's getting me into trouble with my doctor. Help me with this."

I opened up the box and slid out the plastic tray full of wafers and chocolate-dipped shortbread and rolled, buttery sheets and appreciated the surreality of munching on them before discussing L.A.'s history of racial violence. Bobby went for one of the rolled cigars, downed it in three bites, then grabbed a second and let it hang from the corner of his mouth. I nibbled on my shortbread as I looked around the room. Behind Bobby was a bookcase with old photographs of his ancestors. To the right, just like in our house, was a fireplace of shiny, brown tile. A portrait of Malcolm X hung above the mantel.

"Take a closer look," said Bobby, gesturing me up. "You have to excuse me. Hip problems. I've got to stay put." Now that he was seated, he seemed immovable, like a statue of an ancient ruler.

I popped the cookie into my mouth and went up to the picture, which was made of thousands of ink crosshatches. Malcolm was in three-quarters view, pointing off to the left and biting his lower lip midword.

"My son did that when he was fifteen. He's a little older than you now. I always told him to keep up the art, but, you know, there's only so much they listen." He flung a hand in the air. "How's your grandmother?"

"Not so good," I said. "It might be any day now."

"And how's your mother holding up?"

I paused and tried to summon an honest answer.

Bobby chuckled. "It's complicated, I got it. So. You want some ancient history?"

"Yes," I said. "You know, I'm working on the Akai Gurley campaign, to get justice for his family. And we're running up against—"

"What I always explain to people," Bobby cut in, "is that you *need* to say *Black Lives Matter* because in this country, they don't. Not in my lifetime."

"Right," I said, taken aback by the interruption, and the explanation I already knew, but that must've been necessary for Bobby's generation. "Totally." I went on to describe the pro-Liang supporters, the rift in the Asian American community, and the reasons we needed to learn about the Black-Korean Coalition's work. "Maybe you could start with how you and my mom started the Coalition? Is it okay if I take notes?"

"Sure, sure," said Bobby, waving me forward and taking a third wafer. "The fundamental issue here is so-called racism and white privilege. To me, that's it. It's entrenched and engrained." He opened his palm toward me as he talked, pulsing it back and forth for emphasis. "My people have internalized European *values* without access to European *resources*.

On the continuum of Black to white, the closer to white you are, the better your chances of doing whatever you want to do."

"Right, colorism," I said.

"Now, I grew up so-called Creole in Louisiana," he continued, as if he hadn't heard. "We've got to start there." Bobby talked about growing up with six brothers, about leaving Louisiana with his family for Los Angeles "because L.A. schools were integrating. Then, on my first day of high school, I got to campus and the white parents had strung up a row of tar babies."

I stopped. I'd been scrawling along, my hand cramping to keep up with Bobby's fast speech. The image Bobby summoned hovered between us like a ghost and I realized I was holding my breath. Bobby stopped too, wearing a wry smile that almost didn't look pained.

I exhaled. "So that"—I stammered—"so that shaped your understanding of race."

Jeanette leapt up onto Bobby's chair and lay across his lap. He stroked her pink underbelly, which seemed to relax both of them. "The so-called race issue is only a race issue because white people do not want to give up their privilege," he said, starting another torrent of words. "It's hard to deal with that reality, and so they don't. People ask what they can do, but really, *they know* what to do. They just don't want to do it."

He went on like this, letting loose a stream so steady and quick that instead of keeping notes I jotted down key words, though I wondered if I'd ever refer to them, if I could use any of them in our movement. He went back and forth in time: *Trump race-baiting Obama—achievement gap Black students—redlining of South Central—Watts '65—Hillary ignores Black people.* He mixed in details from his life: *stint in army— played trumpet until broken finger—worked as parole officer—raised three children.* He didn't get to the Coalition.

I looked up at Malcolm and his furrowed brow, pointing like he held the millions of unsatisfied people who followed him in that finger, and remembered again the emergency we were in. The country, just like then, was on fire.

"Ah—" I interrupted, trying to sound as polite as possible. "Can I ask you specifically, though, about the Black-Korean Coalition?"

Bobby paused, let his hands fall, and then just as quickly burst forth with a different stream. "Korean-Black problems were intense. It started because Korean merchants and Black residents were at odds. Tensions were heavy—I mean heavy. Shootings." His hands rose and fell like a fountain set to music. "High emotions on both sides."

I interrupted again. "Like, what were you hoping to accomplish? With the Coalition?"

He cocked his head to the side, perhaps annoyed. "We were providing space for people to express themselves," he said, "away from all the bullshit." He held his nose for emphasis.

I smiled at the resemblance between his language and Mom's but still felt impatient. I'd gone to panels with elder activists where, though the speakers were engaging, there were no details about what they actually *did*. I heard stories about how X met Y, I heard grand outlines of the work, but never got the details, the daily life of organizing. I wondered what about activism made it so hard to record.

"So, strategically," I tried again, "what did that mean?"

Bobby frowned at me and then, as if understanding what I wanted, a small smile cracked across his face. "You want the strategies? The analysis?"

"Yeah," I said eagerly. "Like, who were you reading to understand the cross-racial politics of the moment?"

Bobby nodded in confirmation. "Let me ask you this: How much time have you spent in South Central?"

I went blank. I scrambled to form an answer that was both not a lie and didn't prove my ignorance. "Like, recently?"

"Ever," Bobby offered, lobbing me a softball. Then he laughed and wagged his hand. "I'm not trying to put you on the spot. What would an Ivy League kid from the Westside be doing in South Central?" He nodded in approval of his own question. "Same with these politicians who read a poll, then breeze through, talking about how to fix the streets, these academics who've studied the statistics but don't know how to talk to the man working the auto shop. There's your big strategy: go talk to people and find out what *they* need."

I blushed at this simple, most cardinal rule of community organizing, thrown at me as if I'd never heard it. I'd fallen right into the trap of academia, trying to understand this history at a safe, critical remove from the place, from the person right in front of me.

"Totally," I stammered. "We're also all about on-the-ground organizing. That's why, actually, I'm dropping out of college."

Bobby's nose wrinkled. "What's that, now?"

Jeanette's head shot up, ready to meet some danger.

"I'm tired of wasting time in college, going in circles, and want to focus on what you're talking about—the grassroots."

"No, no, no." Bobby wiped the air with his fleshy hand. "Not another young one ready to throw it away. The movement needs people with *skills*, who know how to write, to think."

"Honestly," I said, my voice breaking, "I learn more about that in organizing than in class."

"Uh-huh." He stared at me now, his deep brown eyes magnified through the lenses of his glasses. "You want to ask me the one question?"

I stared back. "What?"

"What's the one question everyone has when they hear about the Black-Korean Coalition?"

I suddenly knew what he meant—it had occurred to me the second Mom mentioned the Coalition. I now had two irreconcilable stories in my head: Mom and Bobby's, and the one everyone knew. And the one everyone knew was so dominant that it was synonymous with Korean America, as in the single time Koreans appeared in my six-hundred-page U.S. history textbook: a shopkeeper standing on an L.A. rooftop, wearing a red polo and the widest grin I'd ever seen on a Korean man, pointing an AK-47 into the baby blue sky.

"Okay," I said. "If you were working on this issue for so long, why'd the tension with Koreans blow up during the riots? Why were their stores burned down, and why did they form militias?"

"Very good question," Bobby affirmed. "You may not like the answer." I looked somber, trying to show that I was ready.

He held up his palm again and ticked it to the side with each word, speaking deliberately. "Whether or not we succeeded was not the motivating factor. We had to do it—had to try."

"If you're not going to succeed," I said, "why try?"

Bobby chuckled to himself silently and his shoulders shook. Jeanette sat up and panted, her long tongue quivering.

"Doesn't that mean I should give it everything?" I pressed. "That you don't know how it ends, maybe, but you push as hard as you can?"

A spasm went through Bobby's body. He jabbed his wafer cigarette in the air. "Young people, these so-called revolutionaries, think they have some key, some big plan that's going to save us. But what it took me a long, long time to understand is that you have to give up winning. Give it up! You think you give up your diploma now, and you're gonna get some other trophy tomorrow. No." He shook his head mournfully. "I watched them burn Watts in '65. I wasn't out there, but I was a young man and I understood in my bones why they did it. You know that kind of knowledge?"

I shook my head, defeated again.

"And then I watched them burn half the city in '92, all the way to La

Cienega. Even when we warned them, and even after all we did. This is a long, long road, and we're not at the end yet. I bet you look at an old man like me and think I figured something out."

His eyebrows arced over his glasses, and I felt my face betraying my disappointment.

Bobby nodded. "It'll probably burn again and again, until we learn the hard lesson." He slid a palm across his face as if to reset it. "Let me ask you. Your mom know about this dropping-out idea?"

"I told her, but—"

"Let me tell *you* something. Your mother. Is one of the best I've met. In all this time, I have met very few who know how to connect with people like she does, who get the *issues* and have *integrity*. She told you to stay in college, didn't she?"

"Yes."

Bobby threw up his hands and flopped back into his big chair. "Well?"

VII

I WAS NAKED, LAID OUT ON A PINK
plastic table like some specimen. A field of droplets gathered on the ceiling and I watched for the next one to swell, fall, and plunk onto me. The man about to scrub me puttered around the table like a surgeon readying for the incision. He sloshed water in a tub and pumped a soap dispenser, then rolled up a little towel and placed it over my groin, a small modesty.

My end of the bargain had come.

Here it was, my body, that alien thing laid out in the open: slim waist, narrow shoulders, no fat or muscle. I fought the impulse to cover myself up, to curl into a ball on the squeaky table. I'd always kept a towel around my waist in the locker room and left my shirt on until the last possible moment at the swimming pool. Even with CJ, back in high school, I'd slipped my clothes off and scurried under the covers.

Don't worry, Mom had reassured me before dashing off toward the women's locker room, *those guys have seen it all.*

I turned to the left, where a handful of older Korean men, retirees with a free weekday, stood in shower stalls. They let steaming water run over their backs and slid rough cloths across their arms and torsos. This,

I understood, was what I might look like in thirty, forty years—they had the same thin frames, their skin draping over narrow bones.

"Hankook?" the scrubbing man boomed. His bald head and bare torso were luminous from so many hours in the steamy room.

I eked out that my mother was Korean, my father was Chinese.

He said something in Mandarin I didn't understand.

I shook my head.

"Korean from China. Like you." He jabbed a thumb at his chest. "English only? Okay!" The thumb turned upward. He grinned and his broad face grew even wider.

It was a little too late for that, I would've explained if I could. He might go back in time and tell my mother to rethink the impossible immigrant dilemma: force the old language into your resentful American child, or accept living in a different world from them. Mom, self-conscious about her accent and not wanting to pass it down, didn't even teach me the basics. She'd stand outside the door and watch Dad read me my bedtime stories, as if being too close might contaminate my standard American English.

Anyway, I wanted to tell him, it wasn't my fault.

The man placed a second towel over my eyes, the way one blinds a horse so it doesn't panic. I inhaled and felt my arm being lifted and pressed against the man's smooth, damp belly. A strong *scrape, scrape* set the nerves on my arm aflame, the hundred small hooks on the plastic mitt digging into my skin. I shuddered but he ignored it, working in steady strokes as if shaving down wood.

"Much, much!" The man lifted the towel so I could see what he held between pinched fingers: a gray worm of dead skin, ddeh. He laughed, a deep-chested bellow that echoed off the tiles. "When was the last time you scrubbed?"

I realized it hadn't been since childhood, when Mom wrapped a hand towel around her index finger and dug it into the soft flesh inside the elbow, the groove of anklebone, the ridges behind the ear. She'd also pause to lift the towel and show off the brown-gray smudges of ddeh, proof that the pain was necessary. Instead, I begged for Dad to give me his mild baths, a metaphor for their styles of love: Mom's harsh exfoliations versus Dad's mellow rinses.

I offered the man a guilty chuckle in response.

He grunted as if to say he'd enjoy this—a real job.

The *scrape, scrape* went on down the ribs, then back up the stomach and chest. He circled the nipples, an oddly touching consideration. He used both hands to dig into the hip crease, another fruitful spot. I peered under the towel to see little brown rolls coming off, like bugs fleeing a flood. The skin on my chest had turned red and splotchy. He moved on to the leg, where there weren't nearly as many nerve endings, and I breathed with relief. It was an education in my own skin.

He folded my right leg and put it to the side like laundry, then moved up the calf and inner thigh. My nerves started to sound alarms as he climbed higher—not believing he would. He did. He lifted the scrotum with the back of one hand while the gloved hand went on as before, an indifferent tool digging up the soft skin underneath. My pelvis jerked to the side but he continued his steady scrape.

There it was: the great shame of Asian American men. A lifetime of bad jokes in movies and teasing in the schoolyard had carved that into me until, one night freshman year, I'd gone home drunk with a white girl, burning the whole way with anger and lust. The second she put a condom on me I drove into her, thrashed, as if to prove something not only for myself but for the whole race. "Okay," she said, tapping my shoulder after a few moments, "I get it." The repulsion and desire flared then hid, covered in layers of dark silence.

Yet another reason, Tiff had said, rolling their eyes when I told them about it later, *to stop fucking around with white girls*. I'd argued that it wasn't liberation, sure, but there was something subversive about the hookup in a society that totally desexualizes us, or else we're always, as Richard Fung said in his article, "looking for my penis." Tiff snorted. *That article. And what are you going to do with your penis when you find it?* They clucked their tongue and waited for my response. *Use it to undo the patriarchy?*

We'd found it, my penis: nothing special, nothing sexual, just something to be moved aside, the way you'd lift a rug to sweep the floor. It was a relief, actually, to let it be a lump of flesh.

"Left side, please!"

The bed squeaked as I turned. I was trembling from the shock of the scrub and I steadied myself against the slippery table like a just-born sheep. Both towels dropped away and I didn't bother putting them back. I'd become a slab of meat, 150 pounds to be worked over like a side of kalbi.

The mitt continued its way along the rib cage, rippling across the bones, then up into the armpit. I giggled and my body shook.

"Okay, okay," he said. "Calm." I sensed that he would tell stories about me later to his fellow scrubbers, the illiterate halfie who giggled like a kid.

"Sit up, please!"

There was nothing left of me to scrub. He draped a towel on my shoulders and clamped his meaty hands over it to knead the flesh there.

"Relax, please. Very tense here."

He was either making fun of me or missed the absurdity of being scraped like a wound and told to relax. My shoulder muscles were hard ridges under his hands. Mom's voice popped into my head, reminding me not to hunch.

He clapped my back, two staccato notes at the end of a performance. Mom, CJ, and this man all demonstrated affection the Korean way: through hitting.

"Finished!" the man bellowed.

I slid off the table and felt the slippery tiles under my feet again. My body shook, and I took my time with each step so as not to fall. The length of my skin hummed, refreshed but raw.

The man grinned and gave another thumbs-up. "Come back soon!" he bellowed. "Much, much." He swept his arm over the confetti of dead skin flaked across the table. He filled a wash bucket and splashed it across, clearing it for the next body, a butcher.

I muttered a weak *thanks* in Korean and ambled over to a shower stall. A small mirror, mounted against the wall for shaving, showed my neck and chest covered in red-pink blotches. My fingers trembled as I lathered the sage-scented body gel into my skin. The peppery oil burned as it entered my open pores.

So this was where Koreans went to unwind.

* * *

I put on the uniform of a baggy T-shirt and shorts and walked into the big, low-lit relaxation room. A muted TV played Korean news, but mostly people lay on the padded floor sleeping or scrolling through big Samsung phones with dangling charms.

I remembered Halmoni babysitting me and, at bedtime, rolling out a blanket next to my parents' bed. *More comfortable*, she said. I insisted on trying it too, but once I lay down I couldn't fall asleep—it felt like the floor was pressing up into all my bones. I crawled back to my soft mattress and left Halmoni, mummy-like, on the hard ground.

I circled the room in an awkward stoop to examine each person as I passed but didn't see Mom. The women lounging mostly had the same neck-length black hair and stocky legs shooting out from their shorts. *Korean moms.* If I surveyed the room, I bet ten out of ten would tell me not to drop out, too.

I lay down on the floor and turned on my phone. A string of texts buzzed, all from Tiff:

> *did you hear?*
> *where are you?*
> *seriously, check your phone*

I opened up Twitter and saw the news trending all over my feed: No jail time for Liang. Judge Chun sentenced him to five years of probation and eight hundred hours of community service, saying he'd be "much more productive" there than in jail.

Probation and community service. I scrolled through and inhaled it all—not only the news but the instant analyses, the condemnations of a system never made for Black life, the exhaustion that bordered on eye-rolling apathy, the precisely worded rage. I read with an edge of masochism, as if pressing a bruise.

I sped through until there was nothing left in my feed and then muttered "fuck" to no one, and no one looked up. I felt queasy, like I'd eaten something rancid.

I texted Tiff:

> *Sorry, I didn't have my phone on me—I'm at a spa*
> *what the fuck?*
> *I thought your grandma was dying*
> *and you were interviewing your mother*
> *No yeah, both of those*
> *It's complicated*
> *there's an emergency meeting tomorrow*
> *Ash is in touch with Aunt T and the lawyer*
> *I'll update you*

Gurley's aunt Hertencia, whom everyone called Aunt T, had never been to a march in her life until her nephew's murder and now was a constant presence, the glue between the family and the organizers. I met her at the courthouse one day as we lined up to surrender our phones before entering the courtroom. Ash introduced us and Aunt T wrapped me in a strong, full-armed hug—the kind of hug you give to family—and thanked me for coming. I was shocked. I was a stranger, and Asian, and throngs of pro-Liang Chinese protesters were outside, but she didn't hesitate for a second. To see this woman go through what she did and still offer a hug like that—that was the moment I knew I had to stay in it.

A form plopped down next to me and I was strangely relieved to see Mom.

"Let me see." Mom picked up one of my arms, still pinkish, and ran a finger across the forearm, like someone examining a wine bottle at a restaurant. "Very soft! You should get scrubbed more often. What's wrong?"

I'd never been able to hide from Mom, but this was one of the few times I wanted her to know. "No jail time for Liang. Nothing. This system will do anything for cops," I hissed, feeling stifled in the quiet room. "He was guilty of manslaughter and criminally negligent homicide, and he gets probation and community service. He'll volunteer at some Chinatown senior center for a few weeks and not shoot anyone else, and that's it."

Mom's lips fluttered. "Well, I'm sure he'll help out there more than he would in jail."

"Jesus, Mom, that's exactly what the judge said. Probably what the conservative Chinese would say, too."

"Ai," she said, "isn't this the son who, last time he was home, was railing about how prisons shouldn't exist?"

I had indeed met some prison abolitionists who showed me that my idea of a "criminal" had been planted in my head by cop movies and political rhetoric, propaganda that actively obscured how the system rammed Black and Brown people into jails and didn't keep anyone safer; I had indeed rattled off incarceration statistics to Mom last time I was in L.A.

Then I remembered the answer Tiff gave when they'd been challenged on this same question by a restorative justice activist. "You have to work with the system you have," I repeated to Mom.

"So *you* get to decide who goes to jail."

"I think we can agree that killer cops should be taken off the streets? That going into people's homes and shooting them should have consequences?"

Mom frowned. "This boy is what, a couple years older than you? Imagine going on trial for all the stupid things you've done."

"No one ended up dead from them."

"Remember your car accident? You would've been in some deep shit if you hadn't been insured and Dad wasn't a lawyer."

I cringed at the memory of that rainy afternoon at the downhill stoplight. I was tired and hit the brakes a second too late and rear-ended the car in front of me. The drivers claimed whiplash and spinal damage, which our insurance company thought was bogus but settled before it got to court. I'd exclaimed my innocence to my parents over and over again: that I'd barely felt the collision, that they weren't even shaken at the time. But, of course, it wasn't about what I'd done or whether there was truth in the claim—it was about us having the resources to control the narrative within the system where my innocence was decided.

"I think you're conflating two totally different things here," I said. "I'm privileged, I get it. And yet, when I try to give up said privilege, everyone tells me not to." I sat up. "You knew Bobby wouldn't support me dropping out, didn't you?"

"How could I know what he'd say?" she smirked. "Did he like the cookies?"

I groaned and slid back onto the floor. My tenderized muscles started to toughen again. "I want to go to South Central," I said. "You both talked about me needing firsthand experience. So."

Mom sighed. "I don't know when we'll have time, with your haircut and all."

"Deal," I said. Our conversations were starting to feel like a high-stakes card game.

Mom slapped my leg to confirm. "Ready for the next step?" she said.

"There's more?"

"Don't look so excited." She pushed herself off the floor and I followed her down a hall with four heavy wooden doors. A sign hung above each one indicating a number.

"Let's start with an easy one," said Mom, opening the door marked *thirty*. The room was decorated with dark rings of crosscut wood and smelled like clean ash. It was hot and I understood that *thirty* indicated the temperature in Celsius. We lay on the straw-mat floor.

"I think I still had a pint of fluid left in me from the yoga class," I said. "I hope this draws it out."

"Try to relax, my son, and inhale. The charcoal is good for you— filters out the toxins."

I looked up at the wood set into the ceiling and walls, skeptical that they would purify us like some human-sized Brita filter.

"So, my son," said Mom, staring up at the ceiling, "what exactly are you going to do with your time, when you drop out?"

"Organize. There's going to be more to do than ever."

"By organize, you mean talk shit about white people on Twitter?"

I turned toward Mom. I did, indeed, say a lot of shit about white people on Twitter. Mom had made an account a few years before, when her friends told her to, until they all ended up switching over to Instagram to share pictures of grandkids and fancy scallop entrées. "You *read* my Twitter?"

Mom pretended to be offended, putting her fingers to her chest. "You keep saying how educational you find it. It's public, isn't it?"

"Yeah, but not—whatever." I turned back to the charcoal ceiling. I hadn't been prepared for our intergenerational conversation to flow both ways.

She sat up and wiped the sweat from her cheeks. "Let's try the next room, now that we're warmed up."

A surge of pride came through me and I was determined to last at least as long as Mom in this Korean dungeon. We exited and I realized I'd always taken the term *room temperature* for granted: a sane temperature at which to keep a room. Mom opened door number fifty-seven.

The walls were made of pink salt bricks and it was so hot the air waved. Mom crunched across the gravel-covered floor and lay down at the far end. I stepped after her and then jerked my foot away from the searing rock. I noticed the pathway of burlap blankets set out for our protection and tiptoed from one to the other, then lay on a blanket next to Mom. Two people lay opposite us, heads covered by towels, still as death.

"How relaxing," I said. The words sounded muffled as the heat filled my mouth and throat like a sock.

"Good to sweat it out," said Mom. She closed her eyes and settled into the rocky bed. "Talk shit about white people all you want, but how are you going to actually build?"

"First," I panted, ready to sweat it out with her, "you need to tear down the old system, which, in this case, is the white supremacist police."

"You're going to do that without a college degree?"

The pink salt emanated heat, pulsing against us on all sides. Sweat started to ooze from my skin.

"Is that less ambitious than stopping violence between Korean business owners and the Black working poor in South Central?"

Mom huffed, as if to say this argument was too easy. "I wouldn't have gotten that job with the city without a degree. And the Koreans, these older men, only respected me because I spoke English, had a job, and went to a good college. That's what they wanted for their kids. So when I said to come to a meeting, they did."

Each breath became an effort. I forced myself to suck in the scorching air then let it dissipate into the greedy heat. "If we aim for respectability politics," I said, "nothing's going to change."

"*Respectability,*" Mom coughed with disdain. "You know, my first job in America was at my uncle's deli. I still remember the pink cleaning stuff he used, because it would burn my throat when I inhaled it. These kids would come in and say things like, *Hey Ling Ling, hand me those cigarettes.* I didn't know what was going on, why they were being that way. I was terrified. My uncle paid me less than minimum wage, but what did I know? I was fresh off the boat. If trying to get out of that shitty life is 'respectability,' then yes, my son, I'm for it."

"I wanted to get a real job last summer, remember?" I said, on the defensive again. "Not the internship that paid nothing, which I could only do because of being subsidized by you guys, like every other privileged millennial. I'm sick of this climbing game, using every advantage, amassing every resource."

"Sure, it's a game. But don't throw the whole board out the window because you're having a tantrum."

I clenched my eyes shut. I'd given up fighting Mom's logic somewhere during my teens, and for years we'd had an uneasy peace, in which I simply tried to slip away from her prodding, in a moody teenage silence. Now it was time to break it.

"If it's less violent than playing, then fuck it, I will throw it out. I'll set it on fire."

One of the people across the room shifted and let out a terse, annoyed grunt. He wanted to sweat in silence.

"And when is it all going to end," said Mom quietly, "if you keep destroying what you have?"

"The revolution."

Mom scoffed. "That's a shortsighted view."

I flushed and my skin was a thin wall pressed by heat on both sides. "Actually," I raised my voice, "revolution is the longest view."

"Uh-huh. And what exactly does it mean? To *you*?"

I paused and thought about where to start—health care for all; an end to racial hierarchy and capitalism; queer liberation. I was probably forgetting something and didn't want to leave anything out. But I couldn't focus in the heat, and without focus I wasn't going to win this argument.

I sat up and felt my sweaty shirt clinging. "I have to go. This heat."

"*Tcha*," tsked the person across the room, eager for me to leave, too.

Mom's eyes were closed, her arms splayed out at her sides, as if to absorb all the heat she could. "There's a cool room next door. Why don't you go, and I'll meet you there?"

I got up slowly and crossed the desert of the small room, tiptoeing back like some cartoon cat. I stepped out and blinked a constellation of yellow spots. I buckled over and held on to my knees as my breath returned. None of the people lying around seemed concerned by this.

I stumbled over to the cool room. It was smaller than the others and covered in white and blue tile. Coils of frost-covered piping lined the walls to underscore the room's theme. It was, essentially, a meat locker. I sat down on the tile, which was so cold it seared my legs.

The sweat evaporated from my skin, turning damp to sticky to dry. Goosebumps popped up on my arms as the moisture turned icy. I shivered. I stood up just as Mom came inside.

"Done already?" she grinned. "So sensitive, even as a boy. It's because you have no padding." She slapped her thigh.

I sat back down, feeling I had to prove something.

"You were going to tell me your idea of the revolution," said Mom with a mix of curiosity and chiding.

"It's too complicated. I can't just say it."

"I have time." She put her leg up on the tile and draped an arm over it, settling in. "If you can't even talk about the revolution, how is it going to happen?"

I shivered again. "It's not that simple." I sat there, staring forward, willing myself to endure the cold. But I couldn't. I stood up. "I'll meet you at room temperature."

Mom closed her eyes and leaned against the wall. "Sure, it's your relaxation, too." She waved her hands under her head. "Hard work taking care of yourself, isn't it?"

VIII

————————————————— DAD AND I SAT ACROSS FROM EACH other in two generic, squeaky rolling chairs in his office. Mom was on a consulting call with one of her nonprofit clients that morning and suggested Dad and I spend some quality time together, especially since my new favorite activity was taking place in a couple hours: a rally.

Poster sheets covered the walls, each filled with bulleted lists and circled words like *Root Causes* and *Mobilizing* and *Feminist Lens?* A couple of smudgy windows looked out toward Wilshire and let in a blue-tinted morning light. Piles of books sent to him from lefty small presses sat in little towers on his desk, on topics like socialism in 1930s Chicago, the bracero program and migration history, and pan-Asian solidarity in nineteenth-century Hawaii. The office was, in short, just like every lefty space I'd been to in New York. Organizers couldn't resist writing big ideas on paper then drawing arrows between them, or keeping piles of books that might inform their work if only they had time to read.

I told him about Liang being let off with probation.

Dad shook his head. "This criminal justice system," he sighed. "It must be a blow. Not to mention the family."

I nodded, thinking of the video of Aunt T bursting out of the courtroom that day, yelling at the reporters, *Akai Gurley's life did not matter! Black lives don't matter!* Pointing down at the floor as if to say, *Take this for your papers.*

Dad gazed a little above and behind me, measuring what he wanted to say. "You know," he said, "we use this organizing tool called a power analysis. I thought it might be helpful for you in thinking through the next steps."

"Don't you need to prep for the rally?"

"I can wing it."

"Sure," I said. Here, maybe, was something I could bring back to Tiff and Ash from my supercool activist parents.

Dad stood up and stuck a fresh poster sheet on the wall. He wrote POWER ANALYSIS at the top in block letters, then drew a rectangle, which he divided in half vertically. His marker made quick strokes, like a practiced artist sketching. Along the left axis he wrote the numbers one through ten in ascending order; at the top of the left side he drew a plus sign; a negative sign on the right:

POWER ANALYSIS

+	-
10	
9	
8	
7	
6	
5	
4	
3	
2	
1	

"Now," he said, "the goal is to understand the situation you're facing, so you can see the most effective places to put pressure."

I was suddenly back in the weekly "family meetings" we had when I was a kid. The three of us would sit around the table and talk about what I'd later learn to call the basics of social reproduction. *Reed thinks it's not fair that he has to go to bed before his favorite shows are on.* Scribble, scribble. *We have a few options: record the show for later, or Reed accepts he'll be tired the next day.* Or, *What's a fairer way to organize chores around the house?* Dad scribbled a bubble chart with dishes, floors, and bathrooms and started writing our initials next to each. *To each according to their needs, from each according to their abilities,* he chimed. It took me a full decade to realize that was Marx. My entire life was an experiment in communal praxis, and somehow my parents were surprised I'd ended up in activism.

"The way it works," continued Dad, "is you lay out all of the different players on this grid according to how much power they have in the situation, from one to ten and how much they're for or against you, left to right."

I laughed. "Which side are you on?"

Dad nodded enthusiastically. "You know, that's a labor song from the Kentucky miners' strike." Nothing energized him like labor history. "Then Pete Seeger recorded it. Now it's being appropriated by everyone, including your movement."

"Yeah, the joke's on us—BLM is actually appropriating a white lefty anthem."

Dad sighed. "That wasn't a criticism. Organizing is all about learning from other movements, even if they're white. So," Dad tapped the sheet of paper, "who are the players?"

"The NYPD."

"And what's been their response?"

"The police chief is 'Broken Windows' Bratton." Ash had held a teach-in where she walked us through Giuliani's brilliant idea to have cops solve all the problems of a neighborhood by giving them impunity to ticket and arrest for the smallest infractions. "He doesn't even want body camera footage released—god forbid they not be able to cover up for each other."

"Okay, so let's say they have a seven for power, and are pretty far against." Dad placed a dot far to the right of the grid, up high, and wrote *NYPD*. "Who are your allies?"

"CAAAV is backing us. You know, the grassroots Asian American organization. And they're part of a whole police reform coalition."

"Good. So they're very supportive, far to the left. And how much power do they have?"

"In relation to the NYPD? Yeah."

"So." Dad put a dot far to the left, at the three mark.

We continued on: the mayor; the media; the conservative Chinese Americans; Black Lives Matter chapters; progressive Asian American groups. My energy sank as the points piled onto the paper. Yes, the *Times* had mentioned us, but only in paragraph twelve of its coverage of the pro-Liang protests: they loved shots of conservative Asians protesting, because media loves nothing more than nonwhite people being racist. The mayor probably hadn't heard of us.

Even some progressive groups were reluctant to come out because the details of the case were too messy: the gun discharge may have been accidental, unlike in Eric Garner's or Michael Brown's cases; it was at night, in a stairwell without video footage; and, of course, it just so happened that the only cop to be indicted, in all the scores of recent cases across the country, was the lone Asian.

We looked up at the finished chart, where a cluster of dots had gathered at the lower left—very much with us, and with little power—while another cluster formed at the upper right—totally against us, with lots of power. My stomach lurched, as if I were on that paper being tipped farther and farther away from power. I wanted to reach out and shake the grid, to redistribute all the dots leftward.

"Well. This is depressing," I said.

"It's not meant to be," said Dad encouragingly, studying the grid like a painting at a museum.

"Was this the point, to show me that these grassroots organizations going up against the courts, the mayor, the police department are bound to fail?"

"Not at all. The next step is to see where you can change the grid: either increase your power or decrease the power of the opposition," he gestured in the air above the chart. "Or, maybe, convince some of them to join you."

"We'll write a nice letter to Bratton and ask him to quit his job and consult with us on defunding the police."

"No, but you could, say, do a media campaign to pressure him to put Liang on probation."

"You don't believe that'll work."

His eyes shifted. "It is a difficult case."

I stood up and walked around the room and looked more closely at the other sheets of paper. I saw this same exercise with other campaigns— saw how, to Dad, this was just one in a thousand happening across the country and how, in his view, it was not the best case, or even a promising one, to spark a mass movement.

I remembered the day in third grade that I came home from school spouting that I wanted to write about Rosa Parks, the first to sit against bus segregation. *No*, Dad corrected me, though he admired Parks, *she wasn't the first*—the NAACP waited until they had the right case in this respectable, middle-aged woman; furthermore, the way the bus boycotts were taught watered down the influence of both leftist politics and

Gandhian satyagraha in order to Mickey Mouse–ify King and Parks and other leaders. My nine-year-old brain broke to reconcile what I was being taught by my well-meaning teacher—white, obviously—and my father, and I wondered whether listening to one would get me in trouble with the other. Some children were told about Santa Claus; I was disillusioned of my movement histories.

"Well, that's the point of being young, isn't it?" I said, trying to get ahead of Dad. "To do something difficult, maybe impossible. That's how movements start."

"Of course. Your mother and I were like that, too."

"But you don't want that for me."

Dad plopped in his chair, which squealed like a crushed mouse. "We want you to do what feels meaningful. And, at the same time, there were some things, looking back, that we would've done differently."

I sat across from him. "*That you would've done differently.*" I repeated, enunciating the vague words, like tapping on a box to guess what was inside. "Like, less radical."

"It's one thing to be reading Gramsci and Mao when you're twenty and have nothing to lose." Dad spoke as if he weren't talking about himself and Mom but some hypothetical young person in the seventies. "It's another to go into the world and actually move people."

"Hide your politics so the system accepts you."

Dad sighed and I could feel that I was slowly rubbing away his cool front—immature, maybe, but effective.

"Of course I wish the world were different," he said. "Of course I'd love to see a democratic socialist state in America. But what we've learned, in this time since the seventies, is how brutally this country treats anyone associated with the word *communist.*"

The word came into the room and, as if it carried an electrical current, charged the air. *Communist.* The old specter still had the power to spook.

"Okay, pause," I said. "All these years, when you were referring to your 'movement days,' you actually meant 'communist days.'"

Dad sucked in air and I saw it was true. A rush of memories came back like restored photographs. Dad had allowed me any sneaker brand except for Nike, reminding me they were made in sweatshops by kids younger than me. I grew up going to Dodgers games but was forbidden from ordering Dodger Dogs because of Farmer John's dispute with the United Food and Commercial Workers. I saw now that this was more than union politics: Dad was constantly calculating how much to insert his radical past into parenting a child under late capitalism, walking a line between full-on consumerism and raising me at a cultish remove from the bourgie norms of my friends.

"Can we acknowledge for a moment"—I stammered, plucking the first injustice that came to mind—"I can't *believe* you let me spend my high school years as an Obama liberal!"

Dad burst into laughter and I saw that this was a little self-centered of me. But I finally understood why they'd always spoken about my organizing with that tinge of condescension.

"What," said Dad, "we were supposed to tell you what hardcore revolutionaries would be doing instead of canvassing for Obama?"

"Something like that."

Dad laughed again. "Reed. As a parent, you watch your child go through a lot of phases. Astronauts, Power Rangers, skateboarding, classic rock. Some stick, but most of them you outgrow."

"So," I said, blushing, "you and Mom were just biding your time until I woke up to how basic my moderate Democrat opinions were."

Dad's lips thinned into an *if-that's-how-you-want-to-see-it* smile.

I leapt up again, agitated, and looked at the poster sheets as if trying to find a way to turn this around. I paused, linking Dad's past to the history I knew. "Wait, did you know, like, Grace Lee Boggs?"

Dad sighed. "Not really. There were a lot of different cadres around then."

"The Panthers?"

"Former Panthers."

"That's cool!" I exclaimed.

Dad's shrugged. "A lot of that history is romanticized."

I felt protective of this new knowledge. "Because this 'radical thing' is always just a phase."

"It's more than a phase," Dad said, still with his infuriating calm. "Our politics back then still inform us. They shaped us. And, at the same time, the revolution didn't come. So we had to figure out what else to do."

"Socialists over thirty have no head?"

"I never believed *that*. The eighties weren't exactly a good climate for leftist politics. There were other things, but"—he paused and reconsidered—"we needed real jobs."

"You didn't have jobs?"

His face closed, giving him time to recalibrate, a talent that won him every poker game throughout my childhood. After I whined and threw a fit a few too many times, he started to go easy on me, but I always knew when he did.

Someone knocked on the door. A young staffer stuck her head in, carrying a pile of flyers and a walkie-talkie. "Oh my god," she said when we made eye contact. "You look just like your dad."

I gave her my best smile. "Thanks? I get that a lot."

"You even sound like him!"

"Just what Reed wants to hear," said Dad. "Time to go?"

* * *

We walked with Dad's coworkers through downtown L.A., the old urban core full of neobaroque and art deco stone buildings abandoned by white flight, then filled in by greasy-spoon diners and clothing stores that had signs only en español. Now, it was turning bourgie again with hipster bars and galleries selling inscrutable, ugly paintings for thirty thousand dollars.

We came upon scaffolding for one of the many new construction projects, and the group veered into the street. Blue tarps and worn camping tents filled the shadowed area underneath, and it took me a moment to understand what I was seeing: a homeless encampment. This was the homeless crisis I'd heard so much about, right in the middle of gentrification. I couldn't stop myself from staring as we passed, at the life made from shopping carts used as wardrobes, cardboard laid down as flooring.

I wanted to murmur to Dad that it was no wonder he'd been a communist, but I didn't want to out him in front of his colleagues.

Broadway opened onto the wide plaza in front of city hall, where a few hundred other union members were gathering. The staffers around me started to join the chant as they approached—*El pueblo, unido, jamás será vencido!*—a basic fluency in Spanish being required for any organizer in L.A. They wore their union T-shirts, all in bold, childish hues of blue and purple and red. Mom's voice rang in my head, *Does being progressive mean you have to dress like shit?* They held picket signs proclaiming, FIGHT FOR 15!

I squinted to look up at city hall, that weird chimera: a white tower crowned by a gray ziggurat like a silly party hat. The organizers had set up a podium on the broad steps, where Occupy had put up a good fight until the LAPD swept them away. Dad walked up the steps to meet the expert handshakes of a couple local politicians, easy to spot with their nice suits and lapel pins. The union officials, on the other hand, had pulled their locals' shirts over their button-ups, communicating that they had power but were using it on behalf of the people.

I wandered over to the edge of the crowd as Dad lined up with the speakers.

A group near the steps pounded on overturned white buckets, giving the event a frantic beat. An old white lefty with a gray ponytail approached me, his eyes cloudy from years of LSD. He handed me a socialist newspaper and offered a fist bump and a "Right on, brother." I thanked him, curled up the paper, and stuffed it in my back pocket.

Dad stepped up to the podium and started the union clap. The crowd put down their picket signs and brought their palms together in a slow, steady rhythm, gradually increasing in tempo until we burst into applause and cheers.

"Brothers and sisters," Dad yelled, the classic union intro. He was in his rally persona: not the quiet person from the dinner table but the fighter. His eyes narrowed and his arms swung in big arcs. "We believe in the dignity of *all work*. We rely on workers to prepare our food, to care for our families, to make our clothes. And yet millions of Californians can't feed their own families on the wages they're given. Is that fair?" The crowd gamely cried *No!* in unison. "Is that just?" Another *No!*

Dad made his pitch for the fifteen-dollar minimum wage and then introduced the speakers. Politicians went first, because they had to leave for other events as soon as possible, then a few union presidents, mixed in with a couple rank-and-file members to give the rally emotional appeal.

It seemed a modest demand, considering the obscene wage gap of current American capitalism. Then I pictured Dad's Post-its and the stack of mean little dots—corporate boards, Republicans in the state assembly, Hollywood and Silicon Valley, even small business owners—opposing the increase. But the campaign was totally sympathetic and had a clear ask, unlike certain others we'd been talking about.

This was how Dad had transformed his past: his pragmatism was its own kind of ideology. It would take someone way off the deep end of the

Left to deny that a few bucks an hour would help working people live. I snapped a photo on my phone and posted it to Twitter.

The crowd began to break up and Dad talked to a couple of reporters. I squatted on the steps and read my socialist newspaper, which reminded me that even though Occupy had ended, the 99 percent was an unstoppable tsunami, ready to crash into the financial system.

Dad came and found me.

"Good job, Dad," I said.

"Thanks, Reed."

That was it—he wasn't the person on the podium anymore. We walked toward Little Tokyo, literally in the shadow of city hall, toward Suehiro's. It was the unofficial spot after every downtown rally because hungry lefties liked getting big plates of down-home Japanese food for cheap. And like Mom, Dad didn't let the Japanese colonizers' history stop him from enjoying their food.

A pile of picket signs had already gathered inside the door. The bright union shirts were huddled all around the light wood tables buzzing about the morning's rally and the next action. Dad and I sat down at a small table toward the back, near the white waving cats. We ordered our tempura combinations from one of the Sansei aunties who, it seemed, had always worked there.

"So back to your communist days."

Dad grimaced like he'd hoped I'd forgotten.

"You all went to get jobs?" I said, picking up the thread from his office. "As in, becoming proletariat?"

He leaned forward, his hands intertwined, a reluctant conspirator. "Yes," he said softly. "We were part of an organization that structured us into different cadres: a group working on miners in West Virginia or factories in East L.A. I ran deliveries for a shipping company in Oakland."

I tried to picture Dad driving a delivery truck, going door to door in a brown uniform. I couldn't, partly because he was my dad and partly because I'd never seen an Asian person who was a native English speaker in anything but a white-collar job. "Did that work? I mean, were people sympathetic?"

"We were a little naive, I think, about going in cold to recruit people. It's not that easy to sit next to someone at lunch and casually hand them a pamphlet about use value and exploitation." He cleared his throat as if to shake that old vocabulary off.

"With the eventual goal of communist revolution? Like, if enough of you organized enough mines, you'd build a mass proletarian base," I felt like some ethnographer who'd only read about this lost tribe and was now finally sitting across from a member. "And then seize the means of production."

Dad groaned as if this were torture. "Something like that."

The old white lefty who'd given me the newspaper came to the table and clapped Dad on the shoulder. He grinned and congratulated Dad on his speech. Mom often joked about the cohort of loco old guys who followed Dad around.

"Thanks, brother, thanks," said Dad, which meant he'd forgotten the guy's name. "This is my son, Reed."

"Right on, Reed!" He missed the cue to give his name, and instead gave me another fist bump, which felt less weird as I realized it was a relic of the seventies that had looped back around to our generation. "Man, what a family. Hey, lemme know what you think of this issue," he said, handing the paper to Dad. The man turned back to me. "You ever read Trotsky?"

"Oh, Reed reads everything," Dad cut in. "See you at the labor break-fast in a couple weeks?"

"For sure, brother, for sure." He fist-bumped Dad, which was so awk-ward I had to avert my eyes.

Dad watched the guy retrieve his picket sign and leave the restaurant. "Watch out for Trotskyites," said Dad. "They're a little bit out there."

"You could be a little more sympathetic, considering your past."

"Some of us outgrew that phase," he said curtly.

"Why, though?" I asked impatiently. "How can you just walk away from the revolution, when that's all that matters?"

"How long has the Gurley case been going?" Dad countered.

"Almost two years," I said, surprised at how long it had been, how saying it made me feel tired.

"We were involved for about twelve," Dad said flatly.

"Twelve years!" I exclaimed. I tried to imagine another ten years of weekly marches, cop watch trainings, community outreach, teach-ins, member recruitment, forming and re-forming coalitions, then my mind stopped.

Something else clicked and I did some math. "Wait, but if you did this for twelve years, and then got your union and city jobs in the eighties . . . how were you organizing in these proletariat jobs while you were in college?"

Dad coughed. "We weren't."

I clapped my hands together and felt a wild grin spreading across my face. I had the urge to jump on the table and gloat, to make my own diagram and draw a big X across it. "Oh my god! You two dropped out of college? You dropped out of college!"

Dad's shoulders went soft, and he seemed relieved, actually, not to be holding the information anymore. "There was this idea," he said slowly, "that education was filling us with bourgeois illusions."

A little montage from the last few days ran through my mind: Mom's coded warnings about the *same mistakes* and *reminding me of myself.*

"So, hello?" I said, waving at Dad as if he were far away. "You guys have no ground to stand on! How can you tell me not to do something you did yourself?"

Dad leaned forward again to subtly suggest we keep our voices down. "The thing is, Reed, I'm not speaking from some moral stance. I know Columbia is a private, pro-status-quo institution. I know you care about your work. I'm not saying it's right or good to go back. But one thing we learned is that life was a lot harder, in the long term, than if we'd just spent another year or two getting our degrees."

The waiter dropped off two huge bowls of white rice piled with panko-crusted squash, potato, broccoli, and exactly two shrimp. I was deflated by Dad's sincerity. Rubbing it in was no fun if he wasn't going to argue back.

"And," I said, not ready to give up my little victory, "when were you going to tell me this?"

"It's not like we wanted to keep it secret—we just didn't know when it was responsible to tell you."

"Responsible?" I scoffed. "Like you might accidentally put that idea in my head?"

Dad gave a tepid smile. "I guess the joke's on us."

IX

"GAH," SAID MOM, REACHING ACROSS the front seat and pushing my bangs to the side, "I cannot wait for Angie to get rid of this mess."

She'd picked me up from Dad's office and drove us straight to the salon, quickly, as if we were in an ambulance speeding against my follicular illness. Signs for panaderias and abogados gave way to Hangul as we entered K-Town—L.A.'s two biggest, swelling immigrant groups butting against each other, giving us the kalbi taco and the modern race riot.

I flipped down the car visor and looked into the mirror to see what was so abhorrent. The sides, I supposed, could have been more even. Little tufts gathered above my ears, and the bangs were growing stringy, no matter how often I pushed them to the side. I flipped the visor back.

"It's not like anyone in the movement cares about these little markers of middle-class refinement," I said.

"Oh please," Mom said. "First off, poor people care about hair, too. Second, half the reason people join movements is to hook up with each other."

I paused and realized that *hooking up* meant coupling in Mom's days, not casual sex. "Yeah, we're saying *blah, blah, NYPD vertical patrols*, and people are checking out my haircut?"

"*Of course* they're checking you out. A smart, handsome young man, and with good politics?" Mom grinned. "You know, you wouldn't be here if it weren't for that."

I gaped at Mom.

"That's right," she said with triumph. "Your father and I met back in our movement days. Here's a little activist history for you."

"Not what I had in mind."

Mom ignored me and cleared her throat. "We held our serious meetings in different places, usually someone's living room. One night, this young Chinese guy was on the hot seat, in front of the room. Everyone was smoking cigarettes and shouting stuff like, *Your father is a bourgeois pig, profiting off the workers of Chinatown.* He was so shy, your father—he sat there blushing and staring at the floor and taking all the criticism. The smoke got thicker, and he had asthma, like you, and started wheezing." Mom tsked. "I felt for him. Plus, he was cute."

"Okay," I groaned. "Thank you for that. But can we talk about this weird communist ritual for a sec? This Maoist denouncement?"

"Ai, just like your father. Skipping to the politics."

"Yeah. Dad told me some more about your 'movement days.' Maybe having gone through this whole bourgeois criticism thing, you might understand me examining my privilege and complicity?"

"That's exactly my point, Reed. Those times fucked up a lot of people."

"But you went to this other extreme! You took me to rallies, like, three times in my youth? And we barely talked about politics. Ever."

"That's not the only way to make change," Mom said with conviction. "We had a few older friends in the movement, so we watched them parent. They'd bring their kids to those all-night meetings, where we stayed up yelling about class struggle. And those kids would be tired and miserable and fall asleep under the table, and they grew up and resented their parents *and* the politics. A few became cold capitalists. So really," Mom said, smiling at her own thought, "you should be thanking us for letting you discover politics yourself."

I remembered the time Mom took me on my college tour to New York and invited one of those movement kids, then in his twenties, to dinner with us. We were crammed around a wooden table in one of those railroad restaurants that felt, coming from L.A., impossibly small—the noise and excitement of the city bouncing between those close walls. He leaned over like some mischievous older cousin and told me how, back in the day, our parents were *crazy*. How his father used to carry a gun. How, whenever the reporters came to one of their rallies, he'd be thrust in the front with a picket sign. "I freaking hated it, man." I kept looking over at Mom, but she neither stopped nor confirmed him, her face neutral like a counselor waiting for a client to wind himself down.

Mom pulled into another strip mall, a sleepy one with a florist, a café, and a mail center. I would've never noticed the salon in the corner, though we'd driven by it all my life. That was L.A.: everything was hidden out in the open, tucked into strip malls so we could play that bourgie game in which the more obscure the strip mall was, the more exciting the find.

I followed Mom inside. A trace of burnt hair hung in the room from a thousand perms. A few hairdressers slouched in their own chairs, leisurely switching between chatting, reading the paper, and scrolling their phones. One of them jumped up and smiled. She was a few years younger than Mom and wore a sensible, flowing blue blouse—something Mom might wear. They exchanged some words, then the woman gestured for me to follow her.

"Angie says you're very handsome." Mom let out a false sigh. "So hard being a mother."

Three washing stations stood at the back of the salon. Angie had me sit in one. When I did pay for haircuts in New York, they were at barbershops: the guy took a clipper to my head with a cursory *How you doin', boss*, did a quick blow-dry at the end, and shooed me out in fifteen minutes. This was something different. I sat down and Angie cradled my neck in the basin.

"Relax," said Angie.

Relax was becoming my K-Town nickname. It was a little ironic, considering Korean people's endemic overwork and alcoholism. I was always almost passing as normal in K-Town, until I didn't bow the right way, or speak a complex sentence, or hold things with two hands. Then I was exposed—an alien in an enclave of aliens.

I heard Angie turn on the tap and felt its mist, then the splash of her hand in the water. Dad used to check the water temperature the same way. I prepared myself for more odd intimacy.

The jet gushed on, so strong it felt like a hand yanking my hair. It soaked through in seconds and Angie shut it off. I heard her giggle and realized I was blinking my eyes rapidly.

Her two strong hands worked shampoo into my scalp and massaged it into a rich lather. The gentle scratching of her nails reaching down to the roots felt surprisingly pleasant, and for once I understood why people paid for a shampoo. I'd never lathered my own hair so thoroughly.

Another blast of water washed the shampoo away. Angie lifted me up by the neck, wrapped my head in a towel, and rubbed it in vigorous circles. She patted my shoulder to get up. I followed her back to the barber's chair and sat. Mom stood by, the three of us looking at each other in the long mirror with my soggy hair clumped at odd angles.

Mom crossed her arms and muttered something to Angie with the intonation of *Please, do what you can*. Angie chuckled. She wrapped me in a barber's cape, tucked it into my shirt, then began sorting my hair with little plastic clasps, planning her attack.

"Who cut your hair?" asked Angie.

"A friend," I said.

"Please," she said, "don't go to that friend again."

"Hah!" said Mom.

Angie's meticulousness almost felt like a betrayal of the haircut Tiff had given me. I remembered my lingering question for Tiff and took out my phone to text them.

> *One thing I've been wondering*
> *If we're still abolitionists*
> *Why are we asking for Liang to be imprisoned?*

An ellipsis appeared in the chat, that Apple-designed simulacrum of human thinking.

> *like I said: we have to work with the system we have*
> *and the family is asking for justice*
> *But "justice" here means Liang goes to jail*
> *Like, if a victim's family wants the death penalty*
> *We follow that?*
> *this is too complicated to get into over text*
> *but yes, in short, that's solidarity:*
> *we stand with the family*
> *Then couldn't we push them towards abolition?*
> *Doesn't solidarity flow two ways?*
> *too much right now, omw to a meeting*
> *talk when you get back*

I slipped my phone back into my pocket and closed my eyes as Angie took out an electric clipper and a comb. Now I understood Mom and Dad's allergy to commands. Anything I told them about my activism—a late night making posters for a rally, working the door at a fundraiser—they'd respond with silence, or a sarcastic remark: *Couldn't they find someone else to do that?* It wasn't, as I'd always thought, because that work struck them as unnecessary—but that they'd taken their share of orders and didn't want me doing the same.

I shuddered as the clipper hummed against my scalp and opened my eyes. Angie didn't need clipper guards but steered the buzzing machine with her comb, and the odd tufts disappeared in an even fade. Mom's friends knew their hair, their spas, their food.

"Better already," said Mom.

Angie put away the clippers and took out scissors. "You live in New York?" she asked.

I nodded.

"My daughter does, too. She's a student. Studying fashion."

The Korean lack of an *f* turned *fashion* into *passion*. "That's a hard field," I said. "Competitive." I wanted to add that it was perpetuating a culture of waste and obsolescence, not to mention racist beauty norms. But we all had our passions.

Angie nodded. "She says it's very lonely. Hard to make friends in New York."

Mom grunted and gestured to the base of my neck. Angie removed the metal clamps, held a chunk of hair between two fingers, and dashed the scissors through to create an even but textured line. Her fingers moved in a fast dance; the metal legs of the scissors twirled and flashed.

"My daughter is interning at Guess," said Angie. "You know Guess? If you need jeans, you can ask her."

"He's not so into fashion," said Mom. "Can't you see? I had to fight to get him here."

Angie nodded with—if I wasn't imagining it—a pained smile, the hint taken. I had to stop myself from laughing. It was impossible to get just a haircut in K-Town: everything came with a side hustle of match-making or gossip. Now Mom was stepping in to protect me, a lioness afraid I was about to be caught in a love intrigue with her hairdresser's daughter and she would later suffer the gossip through the K-Town vine.

"Mom, I think I can handle this. You can sit."

She ignored me and continued watching the progress in the mirror. "Finally," she said, "we can see your face again."

The flurry of scissors slowed.

It was true. The evenness of the top and the slope of the sides made my face look squarer, longer. Angie had somehow managed to stop even the swirl of hairs at the very back from sticking up. Mom had scored another victory: shedding skin first, then hair. If this continued, I would literally be, on the cellular level, a new person.

The hairdresser in the next chair looked over. "Jalsaenggyeosseo!" she said, one of the Korean phrases I knew: "good-looking." A couple others turned around and clicked their tongues in agreement. Mom forced herself not to smile. America was always telling me how I was a sexless drone, undesirable, but here in K-Town I was some long-lost princeling: *So handsome; please, marry my daughter.* Mom had been stopped by cashiers, by random people in grocery stores, by waitresses, who just needed to get off their chests that she had a handsome son. No wonder my Asian American psyche was such a mess: it had to keep flipping between two different realities.

Mom muttered to me, "They're all saying how handsome you are. Like an actor. All you have to do is remove those blemishes." She paused. "If you want, I'll pay for it."

"Cool," I said. "Maybe I can disappear to the motherland for a few weeks, shave my nose down and get double-eyelid surgery, then return for even more compliments from ahjumas."

Mom tsked. "I never said *that*."

I followed Angie back for a rinse, knowing what to expect this time: the jet of water, the strong hands. Tiff and Ash were probably finding Judge Chun's address and recruiting people to vigils, and here I was, being lathered up like a prize dog.

"You know Brooklyn?" asked Angie, rubbing conditioner through my hair.

I nodded. The fluorescent lights haloed her so that her face was dark.

"I told my daughter, Brooklyn isn't safe. Live in Manhattan. But she wants to live there."

"Oh, it's safe," I said. *Not safe*, I knew, being the code word for poor and Black, when it was probably her daughter making it unsafe by raising rents and being ready to call the cops if she felt *unsafe*. "Don't worry."

"Maybe you can help her find an apartment."

I laughed at her persistence. Yes, I could help her daughter navigate Craigslist and maybe give her an introduction to gentrification and anti-Blackness in the Asian community. "Sure," I said. "She can find me on Facebook."

Angie smiled and guided me back to the cutting chair. She snipped at the odd hair, adjustments so fine I could barely see them, then held my head and turned it from side to side to make sure everything lay evenly.

"I admit it," I said to Mom. "It looks better."

"A-hah! You're welcome, my son."

Angie grinned at us in the mirror.

"I mean," I said, "I see how these little projects are meaningful, to a point. Audre Lorde saying self-care is a radical act and all that."

Mom's hands leapt up in exasperation. "Haven't I been telling you that the whole time?"

"Well, I don't think Audre Lorde, as a Black lesbian, was talking about me. Those of us who are East Asian, male, upper-middle class, et cetera, should focus on giving up privilege."

Angie took out a blow-dryer and used it to guide the part right and left.

Mom crossed her arms. "I don't see how giving up privilege," she said, raising her voice over the blow-dryer's scream, "is helping anyone if it just means looking like shit and dropping out of college."

I blinked. Mom had a knack for delivering statements that felt like jabs. But I had a comeback hook. I raised my voice, too, over the whirring machine. "Wasn't allying yourself with the proletariat your version of 'giving up privilege'? Isn't that why *you* dropped out of college?"

The blow-dryer clicked off and the salon fell silent. Mom staggered back half a step. A small push and she would've crumpled. Angie rustled through a drawer, as if not hearing us. I wanted her to turn around, for someone to witness one of the few times I'd tipped Mom off-balance.

"That's funny," Mom said, somber. "Your dad is usually more careful with those things."

"When were you going to mention this?"

"It doesn't change anything," she said, recovering. "That was a different time."

My head throbbed. I looked at myself in the mirror then had an urge to smash it. "You did the exact thing you're arguing against! That's the definition of hypocrisy."

Angie unscrewed a little jar of hair wax. She dabbed one finger in it, then rubbed her palms together. I thought of Halmoni and the pastor and this close touching I didn't ask for.

"This is too much," I said, looking at Angie in the mirror. "I don't need wax, thanks." The shavings on my neck itched. I felt stifled, unable to move my arms. I undid the clasps of the barber's cape and stood, sending a small cloud of hairs wafting to the floor.

Angie tapped my shoulder. "Just one minute."

"I'm not doing anything special today," I said. "I don't need styling."

Mom added her hand to my other shoulder. "Reed. Just sit still for a second, okay?"

My cheek throbbed. It wasn't the gel but the babying—everyone knowing what was best for me. The stylist next to us looked up from her phone with jaded interest. I saw myself from the outside: three people standing in the middle of the salon, two worried women next to a young man with a cape half-wrapped around him who believed some moral axis turned on whether or not his hair was sculpted.

I slumped back into the chair and looked at Angie. "Sorry."

Angie ran her palms across my head, coating the hair evenly in wax, then took small locks between her fingers and twirled them together. She molded the strands in cascades to the right. She was a craftsperson, doing something I'd never have the skill or patience to do with my own head. But that's what Mom wanted me to see: a different level of care.

Angie smoothed down the sides with her palms and twirled a last strand through her fingers so it stayed down. She wiped her hands on a towel. A pang of guilt knotted under my sternum. I wasn't helping anyone by disrespecting Angie's work, when what she needed was to do a good job, get referrals from Mom, and use the tips to put her daughter through college.

"It looks great," I said, with a sincerity that surprised me. "Thank you."

Angie smiled. Mom handed her a couple bills from her wallet.

I attempted a polite bow and thanked her again.

"Come back," said Angie. Then a frown came over her. "Please. Don't let your friend cut your hair."

We got into the car. Orange light washed the sidewalks, the cars, and the low stucco buildings, drawing long shadows across the flat city. Cars lined up in formation, full of people hoping to get home before rush hour, back to whatever it was that allowed them to keep at the grind.

My arguments against self-care, which once felt so watertight, were splintering, leaking. I'd used my small austerities as an ethical stance, feeling I could at least show I was better than the frivolous, basic, and checked out—a weak gazelle worried about not being dead last in the pack. Because as soon as I looked hard at my subject-position I felt a gnawing insecurity, not knowing how I fit into the movement. I could hide under the term *person of color* but always felt, as a nonimmigrant East Asian, only marginally that—shuffled in by default.

Mom and I stared into the low sun refracting through the wind-shield. I appreciated the irony of our situation: Mom wanted me never to repeat her past, and I wanted to be so different from her, yet here we were, in lockstep in a repeat of history.

"Do you regret it?" I asked. "Dropping out?"

Mom was silent for a moment. "It's hard to say. I was a different person then."

"How did you make the decision?"

"It wasn't a decision," she said flatly. "It was an order."

"You didn't organize by, like, consensus?"

"Hah!" Mom cried. "I don't think we knew what that word meant. Did you read about democratic centralism, in all those movement histories?"

I shook my head.

"It's when you take a vote, and whatever the majority decides, everyone shuts up and follows. So one day, the majority voted on this big, puffed-up statement: *It's time to escalate the movement and let go of bourgeois education* or something like that. Of course, most of them had already graduated, so it was really just a fucked-up loyalty test. Just like that, we dropped out. Dad and I packed up his crummy little car and moved down to L.A., where my mission was to politically educate the Korean community."

"Where you hustled part-time jobs and did community organizing, until you got your job at the city on Black-Korean relations," I said, filling out the timeline.

Mom nodded. The sun outlined the clouds in a searing yellow. What escaped at the edges spread across the sky in a blast of rays. My eyes ached and I squinted against all of it. I was scrambling up the hill of Mom's past, trying to gain a footing but falling to the bottom again and again.

"So then, why follow the order?"

"What kind of question is that?" said Mom, impatiently. "Of course we did. That was part of being a good cadre."

I tried to picture myself there, tried to imagine Tiff ordering me to drop out, then summoning the loyalty or faith or recklessness that would allow me to obey. A chiding voice in me said that I wouldn't, and I knew it was true. I wanted to be a radical, but I wanted it my way. I wanted *credit*. Mom knew the unromantic reality of radicalism: to follow an order, to be a soldier, to give up your life for a dream that, when it didn't manifest, meant a lonely lifetime of carrying a decision that no one, not even your child, understood. I was too busy living my individualistic idea of activism—playing with my toy replica of revolution.

X

MOM CARRIED A BIG BASKET OF French cookies into the rest home and dropped them at the front desk. A swarm of nurses appeared, as if someone had rung a bell, and stuffed handfuls of wrapped shortbread into their pockets, gobbled down meringues on the spot.

"That'll be gone in five minutes," Mom whispered to me with satisfaction. "This is how you get good service."

She gestured to a nurse, as if to prove it, and asked her to help us. The nurse followed us with a smile and helped us move Halmoni into a wheelchair.

We pushed her chair into a courtyard. A cinderblock box full of spindly plants took up the center, and wooden trellises that might someday be wound by the bougainvillea creeping weakly up one side provided some shade. It was the kind of half-considered area that almost made me love the city: its lack of pretension, its lazy use of space. It beat sitting in her room.

Mom and I sat on the planter next to Halmoni. We'd wrapped a gray blanket around her lap and a second around her shoulders, even though the afternoon was still warm. Halmoni stared at a bee droning by until it moved out of her range of motion. Her eyes switched over to the struggling bougainvillea.

Halmoni disapproved, I imagined, of the neglected, papery flowers. When she babysat me, she'd spend all afternoon in the garden, squatting with her heels flat on the earth and tsking in disapproval at the lack of care Mom took with the aloe plants, the lemon tree, the tomato vines she'd planted. She tried to impart the basics to me instead, but, being a city kid, I was repulsed by the pale worms wriggling through the soil and complained about my sore legs after a few minutes of crouching. I once cut myself with a spade, and Halmoni didn't go inside for the first aid kit but snapped an arm off the aloe plant and rubbed its gooey guts across the red scratch. I held up my finger, mesmerized, convinced that Halmoni came from some other planet.

Mom opened her big Goyard bag and took out a framed picture. In the photograph, she and her siblings and Halmoni were out to dinner. They were dressed up: Mom and my aunt in floral dresses, her brother in a blue dress shirt with a wide, seventies collar, Halmoni in pearls and red lipstick. A man in a brown suit sat to the right of Halmoni, grinning.

"I was going through some boxes in Halmoni's apartment," said Mom. "I thought I'd leave this with her."

I pointed to the smiling man. "Who's that?"

"Your haraboji," said Mom.

The air stopped in my throat. Of course he was Mom's father. He had the same round face and button nose. Haraboji: the branch that had split off of Mom's stunted family tree, who had died somewhere in Korea sometime before I was born. All I knew about him fit into one breath: he was a kessuge, son of a bitch; he was an alcoholic; he was abusive—in short, Mom said, a typical Korean man. In the photograph, his face was swollen and pockmarked, presumably from years of Johnny Walker, and three of his teeth were gold.

"I thought you never saw him again after you left Korea," I said.

"That's mostly true."

I didn't, to my surprise, feel indignant at not knowing my grandfather's face. I felt a sad clarity, like waking up after a pleasant dream to a cold morning. "You know," I said quietly, "I always had this idea that one day I'd ask Halmoni about her life. And now that's never going to happen."

"You want to know?" said Mom, her jaw hardening.

I nodded, though I wasn't sure I did.

"I guess I should start in Korea," said Mom, "around the time Haraboji was drinking and beating the crap out of Halmoni. I can still see the bruises on her face—all purple and yellow."

Mom stared at nothing like some shaman readying a rite. It felt as if the floor were opening, lowering us into a pit. I braced myself as I strained to picture this ancient history—Korea, Halmoni's bruised face, this strange man—that was not so long ago. Halmoni continued tracing the bougainvillea with her eyes.

"One day she left," continued Mom. "Halmoni left Korea without telling any of us. I remember sitting on the stoop, crying and crying, wondering when she was coming home. How's that for being a mother? *Tuh*," she spat, as if answering herself. "Haraboji, meanwhile, was drinking and losing apartments. One time, he disappeared, probably to some mistress's house, and we were evicted. So me and my siblings had to put all of our shit into a little cart and push it down the street, with nowhere to go. Then it snowed, and we started bawling." Mom let out a sharp laugh. "We must've looked fucking pathetic."

I sat on my hands and let my weight press them into the rough cinderblock, needing something hard to ground me. I couldn't have forced a laugh if I tried.

"It took Halmoni a couple of years to save up the money to send for us. I don't want to talk about that time," Mom snapped, though I hadn't asked. "I'll never forget the day she finally sent a plane ticket to America. My uncle interrupted class, and everyone stared at me like I'd won a prize, passage to the beautiful country.

"Of course, we got here and Halmoni was working as some rich people's maid. All she had was this tiny apartment in K-Town."

"But you left Haraboji in Korea."

"Yes." Mom stared at the photo. "We assumed he'd drunk himself into a hole or gotten remarried. Then one day, years later, he showed up at our apartment in L.A. and knocked on the door during dinner, no warning, smiling like it was some big fucking reunion.

"Halmoni stood there and cussed him out: *You kessuge, you alcoholic.* But, of course, she let him in eventually." Mom glared at Halmoni. "We went out to this big dinner that night. That's where this photo is from. Haraboji spun all these stories about working for a Korean shipping company in Saudi Arabia, shaking hands with millionaires. Said he was rich. And you could see Halmoni's mind running, making a shopping list. For a second, I think we believed all the bullshit. Like we were going to be a family."

Mom rubbed the photograph's frame with her thumbs. "I'm fuzzy on the details because I went back to Berkeley. I'd get these postcards from Halmoni: Paris, Madrid. Their second honeymoon. She was talking about sending your aunt to private school, moving to a big house on the Westside. Halmoni grew up rich, right, so she always expected that life to come back.

"Then, a few weeks later, she felt a lump on Haraboji's throat. It was cancer. Halmoni wanted him to go to an American hospital, but Haraboji insisted the health care was better in Seoul, and he was a big man now with connections. So he flew back, checked into a hospital, and died. Halmoni only got the notice afterward. I don't know if she spent more time crying or cussing out the kessuge.

"When she went to claim her part of the will, Haraboji's sisters said, 'What money? He was broke.' So Halmoni used one thing she learned in America: she sued. She went back and forth to Korea looking for documents and hiring a private investigator to get all this money he supposedly had. But they painted her in court like the jealous widow, which, let's be real, she was. In the end she got nothing."

Mom stopped and the little courtyard was silent. The sun was setting and the light turned the stucco walls a dull blue. I noticed I'd been taking shallow breaths and felt dizzy. I let out a long exhale.

It was the most Mom had ever said of her life before America. No wonder she wanted to start her story the day she arrived, to sever everything that happened back there.

Mom held the photograph to Halmoni's face. "Remember this dinner?"

Halmoni's head jerked forward and her eyes went fiery. The monitor on her armrest beeped and a yellow light flashed. "Kessuge!" she spat, a dab of saliva forming at the center of her lips. Her neck strained, like she was ready to bite the picture in two. "Kessuge!" she rasped again, shredding the word in her throat.

Mom and I lurched back. The shrubs in the planter poked my neck.

I looked at Mom and we exchanged dumbfounded expressions. Then Mom's eyes watered and she exploded into laughter. Her whole body shook, as if Halmoni had told some amazing joke. She heaved a breath so that she could howl with more laughing. A nurse poked her head into the courtyard but Mom shooed her away.

Finally, Mom wiped her tears, her shoulders trembling. "So much for leaving this photo by her bed. I think it would give Halmoni a heart attack."

The monitor dinged again, then stopped. Halmoni settled back onto the wheelchair. Her eyes darted between us, as if asking what the joke was. I wiped my palms on my jeans. They were sweating.

Mom handed me the photo. "Since you want to know so much about your history."

Haraboji smirked at me like a gargoyle. I thrust the frame back at Mom. "I don't want this."

Mom glanced up in surprise. She took the photo gingerly.

"What the fuck," I said. My head burned with a pressure pinching inside my skull. "I don't see what's funny. I don't want this person's face on my wall. What kind of abusive, patriarchal—"

Mom put her palm on my leg softly. "I'm only telling you because you asked," she said.

"Not about this, though. I wanted family stories about activism, not stories of violence and worshiping money and lying."

My eyes burned and I saw my immaturity but couldn't manage anything else. Mom nodded and looked away, not out of coldness, but because this was a feeling I had to go through on my own.

We were silent as we wheeled Halmoni back to her room. I scooped her up by the shoulders as Mom lifted her legs. My grandmother's bony back pressed against me, this delicate body that had survived her dog of a husband, my grandfather. We lay her down on the bed. I wanted to say goodbye, but her face was drained and soft, her eyes already closed.

XI

I SAT IN THE BACK SEAT OF A BLACK Toyota speeding toward K-Town, one of the rideshares flooding the streets on Saturday night. I hated participating in the gig economy, but L.A.'s architects left me little choice when they gutted public transit decades before I was born. That was the consolation prize of late capitalism: freeways, free market, free rides if you recommend the ride service to a friend.

CJ's high school friend was *getting us into a club*, which was stupid, but I needed to see CJ and talk about everything I'd learned. Plus, we were finally twenty-one, finally able to have a drink without going to an underage sojujip, getting in with CJ's sister's ID only to be overcharged for the contingency of the owners being busted.

The driver dropped me off in the lot next to the club, a windowless two-story box on Western. Two doors led inside, one with a long line of the subaltern clubbers, the other for the normatively beautiful and very rich to breeze inside.

I stood in the lot scanning for CJ. I took out my phone, because I sensed this was a situation where only sociopaths just stood around without something in their hands. Two-thirds of the people in line were scrolling too, a row of faces made ghostly by the white-blue of screens. A few snapped selfies to show their friends how much fun they were about to have.

I felt a slap on my arm. "Oh shit, it's you!" said CJ. "You got a haircut. I was like, *Who's that stylish dude in the corner?*"

I could almost hear Mom laughing at me. CJ gave me one of her quick, strong hugs and I smelled a new perfume on her, jasmine plus something smoky and expensive. Her dress hugged her body in a series of neat, mesmerizing maroon pleats.

"Nice dress," I said.

"Thanks, boo. This rich girl I was kind of seeing gave it to me before she broke it off because I was 'too intense.' Anyway, I'm keeping it—it's vintage Chanel."

I looked again and could see the fabric had a sheen and weight that the average college party dress did not. "Fancy," I said.

"Please." She opened her clutch and swiped through her phone. "I'm waiting for Jane to text me back. She's fucking the DJ."

I blinked and felt out of place. I hadn't seen Jane since high school and I didn't know clubs really operated like this. CJ, though, had always been able to span two worlds. She was the Harvard kid who read Joyce but also smoked cigarettes and hocked loogies standing next to white Civics in parking lots. She had even attended a Korean megachurch until sophomore year, when she found Nietzsche. I'd found the term *code-switching* funny when I learned it in college: to me, it just described how my high school friends got through the day.

"Jane's in a car. Let's drink some." CJ nodded at a dark corner of the parking lot near a dumpster.

She took out a flask and gulped down a mouthful.

"Isn't this a little flagrant?" I asked.

She rasped from the burn of whatever she'd just drunk and wiped her mouth. "Who's going to stop a Korean girl in a dress outside the club?"

I remembered going with CJ to CVS once, when I hadn't known her that long. She removed a stack of facial wipes from their expensive-looking box and stuffed them in her purse, then waved at the cashier on the way out. I nearly gave us both away with my gawking. She explained to me outside that this was the one upside of being an "innocent-looking" Asian girl, a small consolation for the steady barrage of harassment she endured in public.

"So we're going to abuse our East Asian privilege when people are killed by the cops for less than this."

CJ took another sip and rolled her eyes. "Can you stop with the white guilt?"

"How can *I* have white guilt?"

"You tell me—in that *Frasier*-ass social justice language you use now."

"Unlike your appropriative AAVE."

"Bitch," she spat, "I talk how I talk. You're just afraid to say the wrong thing around Black people."

"I—" I felt my mouth open and shut, like an automatic door malfunctioning.

CJ fluttered her lips. "I'm just fucking with you," she said, unconvincingly. She grunted and thrust the flask at me.

I took a swig. It was vodka cut with a touch of orange juice, and the combination tasted like gasoline. We stood there in silence, watching black Toyotas pull into the parking lot, drunken Korean kids stumble out, compose themselves, and stride toward the entrance.

I took another gulp and screwed up my face. "Okay, my bad," I said. "If I'm in a mood it's because I took your advice and asked my mom about her past, and now I feel like I'm losing my shit, like I'm falling into some bottomless hole."

CJ nodded slowly.

"Do you ever feel like everything you say to your mom," I continued, "it doesn't matter, because the shit she went through was so painful? Any point I argue, my mom shoots it down with some terrible new fact about her past."

"Dude," she said, "welcome to my entire fucking life." Her hooded eyes, made heavier by mascara, gave her expression a classical drama.

I scanned my brain for the right thing to say, to break through the quiet—something that would help me, help both of us, understand a way out of the deadlocks with our Korean moms. But nothing came.

CJ's phone buzzed and her eyes popped open. "She's almost here." She offered the flask to me. I shook my head, already fuzzy-headed and disappointed we weren't going to talk more. CJ tilted her head back, chugged the rest down, and let out a gravelly belch. She smiled with dopey satisfaction.

A silver Cadillac pulled into the parking lot and Jane got out. I'd always wondered who would pay extra for a luxury rideshare and now I understood: everything about the club rested upon appearance, starting the moment you entered the sight of the bouncers.

"'Sup, bitch!" yelled Jane as she walked out, her arms flung into a wide V. Her blue dress was cut to show her left shoulder and her hair flowed outward in lightly curled waves, like in a commercial. This was not the high school girl I remembered with her baggy jeans and white tank top. CJ gave a little yelp, ran over to Jane, and wrapped her in a hug. The two of them rocked each other side to side as they embraced, like wrestlers trying to tip each other.

"Oh hey," said Jane, turning to me. She hugged me lightly as if I were her cousin. "The Ivy boy is back."

I tried not to feel awkward about touching her bare shoulder. "Thanks for, like, getting us in," I said.

"It's whatever," she said. She looked me up and down and didn't hide her disappointment at my outfit. "Nice haircut. I'll be right back." She gave the bouncer a hug and went into the special door.

I nodded at the entrance. "Of course, in late capitalist leisure, even the doors are built to enforce class distinctions."

CJ groaned. "You sound like Adorno if he, like, worked out his ideas on Twitter."

"I'll take that as a compliment?"

"Ugh, who would want to be friends with Adorno? Sounds depressing as fuck."

"Horkheimer?"

But CJ was already walking over to Jane, who waved at us from the special door. Jane handed us each a blue wristband. I looked at the other line and saw that they were getting yellow bands. We were like farm animals graded and split into troughs.

We walked inside and the music slammed into my body, thudding to the bone like a car crash. I couldn't make out the ceiling in the cavernous space, and the spinning lights made it hard to orient myself—there was no center to the room, no clear exits, just a bright dance floor off to the side. A few clusters of people stood at its edge, looking bored or predatory. A must of sweat and alcohol pressed into my nose, swirling with the floral notes of many perfumes.

"So this is a club," I yelled at CJ over the music.

"Whoo!" She shimmied and threw her arms up.

I envied her absence of self-consciousness and knew I could get there, could release the churn of thinking and act like a normal millennial. I only needed more substances in my body.

Jane led us to a bar in the back, where racks of booze were lit from below and bartenders gripped inverted bottles between their knuckles. It was still early: a few dozen people halfheartedly swayed around the dance floor, sipping drinks to do something with their hands or trying to make meaningful eye contact with one another. A second story rose above the dance floor, ringed by black leather booths for people with money.

Jane went up to a guy with a shaved head and hard, angular face—the kind of Korean guy I avoided in high school, the kind of bro Peter Liang reminded me of—and planted her mouth on his.

"This is my boo, Austin," she yelled, over the music. "This is my high school bestie and her—friend."

"'Sup," said Austin, in the low growl of K-Town bros. His white button-down glowed in the dark club, and the points of his collar looked like they could slice vegetables. He hugged CJ and swiped my hand.

"Hey, thanks for getting us in," I said to him. "When's your set?"

"Two," said Austin.

"In the morning?" I checked my phone. It wasn't eleven yet.

He smiled, amused. "This place doesn't get going until midnight, at least."

A woman with a headset came up to us. She glanced at Jane, with her arm around Austin, looked past me, and then went over to CJ. The two took turns talking into each other's ears.

"Later, fools!" said CJ. She gave me a little shove. "Get some drinks and loosen up, Adorno."

"Have fun, girl," said Jane, waving.

CJ disappeared into the crowd with the woman. I asked Jane where they were going.

"Booking," said Jane.

It felt like a blood vessel burst in my brain as I remembered the warnings Mom had given me of the seedy side of K-Town, where women were brought to tables to pour drinks for men and laugh at their jokes, all with the hint that there was more to come. "That's actually a thing?" I yelled over the music.

"It's not even like that," said Jane. "I've done it a bunch—it's just free drinks."

"You better not be doing it anymore," cut in Austin.

He wasn't smiling but Jane gave him a little slap on the chest as if it were a joke. Then she turned to me. "Why don't you buy your unni a drink?"

"Oh, yeah, sorry," I muttered. I knew I'd be considered ruder if I weren't a clueless halfie. I leaned forward on the bar and yelled our order at the bartender. I didn't want to know the punishing amount they charged, so I handed over my card.

I gave Jane her cosmo and sipped my gin through the tiny red straw. Austin leaned an elbow on the bar and wrapped the other arm around Jane, absent-mindedly stroking her shoulder like one would pet a cat. "So," he said, "you're at Columbia? You gonna be an I-banker, make some paper?"

I chortled. Then I composed myself. "Sorry," I said. "No."

Austin's eyes narrowed. "Why would you spend all that money on Columbia, then?"

I saw that we'd have to dive into a minihistory of the Gurley case, then talk about Asian Americans perpetuating anti-Blackness, in order to arrive, ironically, at an agreement that it wasn't worth the money to continue my education. "I guess I wanted to get away from L.A. for a minute," I said instead.

"What's wrong with L.A.?" asked Jane, blinking.

"No, nothing. Just, if you don't leave the place you're from, how do you figure out what to do? How to have the biggest effect on society?"

"You and CJ freaking overthink *everything*." Jane extended her index finger and poked the side of my head. It hurt. "Anyway," Jane continued, "what's up with you two?"

If she saw me blushing, I could always blame it on the alcohol and

Asian glow. Half the clubbers were red like lanterns. "What do you mean?"

"Yeah, she's pretty cute." Austin nodded sincerely. "Knows how to dress. Not a lot of smart girls do."

Jane gave him a weak slap as if to say this was a little sexist, even for her. I gripped my plastic cup and felt it crack at the edges. It was already empty. I ran my finger against the edge and felt the sharp point where it broke.

"Hey," I said, "who needs another drink?"

Austin nodded. "Let's do some flaming homos."

"Excuse me?" I said.

"They're super fun," chirped Jane.

"That's a little problematic." I raised my voice to make sure they heard me.

"I got nothing against gays." Austin's jaw went slack, as if an idea had struck him silent, and his head swiveled toward me. "Are *you* gay?"

I couldn't tell if he was being sarcastic or just felt uncomfortable asking. "That's not the point. I mean, even if one conforms to heteronormative sexuality, it's still your job, as an ally, to oppose homophobia."

Austin turned to Jane. "Is he gay?"

He was making fun of me. "Forget it," I said. "Let's just drink, yeah?"

I forked over my card again and the bartender set up three small glasses on the counter and filled them with some dark mixture, then placed three shot glasses behind them. He poured an amber alcohol into the shot glasses and touched a lighter to them, sending a slow, blue flame crawling across the surface. He warned us to be careful. It struck me as a terrible idea, and possibly illegal, to light things on fire for drunk people to pour down their throats. But K-Town was outside the law.

Jane handed me a cup and shot glass and counted down from three. I did what they did: blew out the flames, dropped the shot glass into the cup, then downed the whole mix in one go. It had a caramelized after-taste, oddly like Coke.

"That's not bad," I said.

"Check it out," Austin grinned, "he loves homos."

"A wordsmith," I said.

"Play nice, boys," said Jane.

"When is CJ getting back?" I asked.

Jane flipped her hair over her shoulder. "That's your boo."

Austin glared across the room and jerked his chin to get our attention. He let out a disgusted *tsk*. "I hate it when Korean girls date Black dudes. Like they're so fucking proud of it."

I followed his gaze to where the target of his hatred was leading her date toward the dance floor. Both of them stared forward intently, as if they were walking through a storm.

I wheeled back to Austin. "What the fuck."

"It's not that there's anything wrong with it," Jane said delicately, as if explaining something sad to a child. "But, like, why the eff do you need to parade it around K-Town?"

I spoke in a low, steady voice to stop myself from yelling. "Do I seriously need to lay out how racist that is."

Austin turned to me and his neck disappeared under the dead weight of his head, which he tilted back at the precise angle that meant he was ready to fight. "Step back," he said. The words came from the very bottom of his throat, like a bass drum.

Though I wanted to scream at this ogre, wanted to dismantle his Neanderthal world view, a primal part of me knew that this conversation would end with fists—and that mine would lose.

I turned away from the bar and scanned the club. The swirling lights and pressed-in bodies seemed to have multiplied. I chose a direction and started walking.

"Get your girl!" Jane yelled after me.

I waded through the crowd, muttering a constant awkward mantra of *excuse me* as I shouldered through groups of people. I began to sense that it wasn't acceptable for a guy to be alone, pushing through—that I was the definition of *creeping*. And I might have felt embarrassed if I were sober, if I weren't driven by disgust at these friends of CJ's and my powerlessness to say anything to them. I began shoving through with purpose, relishing the annoyed grunts and side-eyes directed at me.

I climbed a set of dark stairs. The bumping music sounded distant, like I'd swallowed speakers that were pulsing weakly from my gut. I listened and thought it might, for all I knew, be the same song as when we entered, which didn't say much for Austin's vocation.

I leaned against the railing and almost saw the appeal of the dance floor, a mass of limbs polished red, blue, and gold by the lights: To lose yourself in the sweating and gyrating, an abandon built on unspoken racial exclusion, because wasn't that our right as people who had been excluded ourselves? If you could ignore or deny that, it might even be fun.

I spotted CJ at one of the booths across the balcony. She sat across from another woman, with three men between them. She held her elbow with one hand and poured a frosted bottle of vodka for the man sitting next to her, his hand on her thigh. The whole group did a shot together and laughed. I walked over.

"Oh hey!" CJ looked up with an annoyed smile. She introduced me to the others.

I didn't pay attention to their names. "Hey," I managed. "Nice to meet you." No one shifted or offered me a seat.

"I'll be down in a minute," said CJ.

"Another!" said the guy in the middle. I squinted in the dark at his lined face and fleshy cheeks. He was easily forty.

"What is this even?" I said to CJ, but loud enough for all of them to hear.

"There a problem?" Fleshy face glared at me.

CJ forced a laugh. "My friend's drunk. I'll be right back." She stood up and gave me a little shove on the chest with both hands. "Stop talking," she said, quiet but firm.

We pushed through the crowd again, CJ leading me by the shoulder. Her hand was warm and I was embarrassed by how comforting it felt.

We stepped outside and my ears rang from the sudden quiet. The desert air picked up and I realized I was sweating through my shirt.

CJ spun around to face me. Her eyes were luminous under the orange sulfur lights. "I hate it when I have to babysit you," she said.

"Your friends are fucking racist." I described what happened while she was gone.

"It's a club." CJ rasped. "I'm sorry you had to be with people who don't share your exact politics for ten whole minutes."

"I don't think I'm being picky if I don't want to be around people who are against interracial relationships."

CJ scoffed. "In that case, you don't want to be around my mom, my aunts and uncles, my grandparents, most of fucking K-Town. And yeah, I don't agree with Austin, but I saw that couple too, and it's obvious that bitch just wants attention."

"Cool—so we just smile and nod at all the anti-Blackness in our community, the way you smile with those creeps in that booth who just want to fuck you?"

"Because I should actually be sucking off you and your brilliant theories instead, right?" she screamed. "I'm fucking sick of you reading Twitter and saying the same shit everyone else is so you can feel superior—so you can 'save' me by showing me the truth."

I reached toward CJ by reflex, because even though I knew it was ridiculous, that was exactly what I wanted: to take us away from this place for somewhere better, purer.

She swatted my hand away. "Don't *fucking touch* me." She swung her knee up, then slammed her foot into my shin like she was trying to kick down a door. Her heel dug into my flesh and I yelped and stepped back.

CJ panted, ready to do it again if I came closer. We were crouched like dogs spoiling for a fight. Then she spun around, flashed her wristband to the bouncer, and went back inside. A few clubbers looked up from their blue screens and I felt like some gladiator performing for them. I blinked and limped toward the entrance, my shin burning as if a hot iron were pressed to it.

Jane appeared at the door, blocking the way and smiling with malice. She'd seen the whole thing. "Let CJ get dicked down by a stranger if she wants, yeah?"

"That's disgusting," I said. "I just want to talk."

"That's what they all say." She pouted sarcastically. "I thought you two *weren't even a thing*."

My mouth tasted sour and I felt like vomiting. "You're already racist. Don't be a bitch," I said.

I regretted it immediately and the nausea roiled up.

Jane's eyes popped open and her smile spread sharply. She looked delighted. "Look at the Ivy boy—a feminist ally, too!" She turned to the bouncer and placed two fingers gently on his arm. "Oppa," she said, *older brother*, "don't let this douchebag in." She disappeared into the dark of the club.

I made eye contact with the bouncer, his face weathered and pale like a radish. There was so much jaded pity in his eyes—it was clear that he'd seen this exact scene thousands of times—that I turned away.

I reeled like I'd just stepped off a carnival ride. I walked quickly away from the club, as if I might outrun what just happened. I lengthened my stride and let each step crash into the hard concrete, sending a shudder up through my knees. I wanted the steps to hurt.

I paused under a streetlight and rolled up the cuff where CJ had kicked me. A few inches of skin were red and peeling. The first yellowy hints of the bruise to come flowered around it. I pressed the wound and the scalding pain was a nice distraction.

I let go and kept walking. If I couldn't outrun the embarrassment, maybe I could grind it numb. I did it most nights in New York, wandering up and down the island, stalling before bed because I knew what waited for me before sleep: rehashing the day's small failures, the tally of ways I'd fucked up in friendship, in the movement, in doing my part to chip away at the carceral capitalist machine we lived in.

A dry breeze pushed the smell of dust and night jasmine across the flat city, and the cool air felt good on my face, still clammy and glowing from alcohol and shame. The streets near the club were deserted, diamond grates pulled across the dead storefronts. The ringing in my ears faded. I'd reached the edge of K-Town.

I tripped on a broken sidewalk, cracked by a tree root. I muttered a little curse at the neglected pavement and this pedestrian-hostile city. I kicked the crack and a tiny flake of cement rubbed off. I kicked it again and again, reveling in the gray grains that rolled away, until my toe throbbed.

I took out my phone and called a rideshare.

XII

A SHARP RAP AT THE DOOR WOKE me up. The morning light bludgeoned my eyes and my throat felt like I'd swallowed sand. I glanced at my clock and the red lines glared at me, informing me it was once again past ten.

The rapping came again. "Did you still want to go to South Central?" asked Mom through the door.

I stumbled into the dining room, where a frothy green smoothie sat on my placemat, made with Mom's new high-powered blender. I sipped it and felt its promise of renewal, the vitamins edging me back from oblivion. Underneath, though, my insides ached from the alcohol, and a drum of guilt pounded away.

Mom appeared at the door. "My hangover cure," she said, holding up her own glass of green liquid. "It has turmeric. More partying with CJ?"

"Not exactly," I said.

"You look like hell," said Mom. "Keep sleeping. We'll go another time."

"No," I said. White light soaked the blinds of the dining room, announcing another cloudless day. "This is important. Just give me, like, fifteen minutes."

I made a double dose of coffee from the machine and drank it standing in the kitchen. It infused me with a bright, hollow energy. I was like a zombie, reanimated by chemicals, which was exactly why everyone drank coffee all day at their cubicles: to force their bodies into the repetitive motions that greased the machine, *zombie* originally a word for the eerie act of walking to and from work. CJ's voice came to me, telling me to shut the fuck up, Adorno.

* * *

The morning had already turned hot, the yellow sun burning its small, bright hole through the blue dome. A wisp of clouds hovered in the west. Another problem with L.A. was that no matter how shitty you felt, the days were relentlessly sunny. New York gave you the bitter gray to match.

"I can drive," I said to Mom, in the driveway. "Since I suggested the outing."

She looked skeptical but handed me the keys. I backed the car out, glad to have a distraction from the embarrassing scenes of the night before replaying in my head, from the aching bruise on my shin.

We drove back down La Brea. A strip mall, with its white, faux–art deco facade caught my eye. I remembered when it was a fenced-in lot, filled with rubble. There were lots like it all over Mid-Wilshire and K-Town during the nineties, remnants of the riots that no one wanted to touch. I was like some washed-up detective, seeking one little piece of evidence that lay, absurdly, in the middle of one of the most recorded events in recent American history. But if my hunch was right, it was buried because of its potential power—an example of cross-racial solidarity that would blow apart the narrative that our communities were always at war with each other. I felt a little flash of hope.

I merged onto the 10 freeway, pushing the fuel-efficient engine to catch up with the cars zipping by. It was always a little rush to be back on the freeway, to float above the city. The monotony of the flat buildings dropped away, and instead we saw palm trees pricking the sky, the San Bernardino Mountains emerging from the smog like gray ghosts.

"So," said Mom, "where did you want to go?"

"I was thinking you could just show me some of the sites where you and Bobby did your work. On the Coalition."

"Oh, god," she said. "It's been so long—all these podunk little churches and delis."

I sighed. I hadn't made a plan, and either Mom was being evasive or had actually forgotten. I kept driving anyway.

The freeway banked as it approached the huddle of downtown, as if the engineers hadn't counted on actual tall buildings in L.A. and had to reroute at the last minute. I merged onto the Harbor Freeway as it dipped below street level, moving through urban renewal's legacy, which, instead of "renewing," sliced up Black and Brown neighborhoods with six lanes of concrete.

"We could go to Watts Towers," said Mom. "At least it's something to look at."

"Honestly," I said, "I've never been."

"Not even on a school trip?"

I shook my head. "I mean, you sent me to school on the Westside, so we went to the Getty, not Watts."

"Watts Towers ain't the Getty."

"Isn't that the point? The neighborhood is underresourced, so it's impossible to imagine a Getty in South Central. And actually, if it were there, it would probably just create neocolonialist dynamics that didn't benefit the neighborhood."

"Are we going or not?" Mom asked.

"Sorry, yes." I was picking fights, the outing mixing poorly with my headache.

I pulled off the freeway and Mom handed me her phone. "You do the thing," she said. I tapped in the location and a mechanical voice directed us through a residential area.

I turned onto a cul-de-sac and they appeared right in front of us: a cluster of hollow structures shaped like elongated Christmas trees, made of steel bars and ceramic shards set into concrete. They were weirder and smaller than I'd thought, the kind of thing you'd find in yards with lots of cats and overgrown spider plants.

I parked and we got out. A white metal gate circled the towers, announcing that they were closed for restoration. Single-family homes sat just across the street. A woman came out to check her mail, glanced at us, accustomed to strangers, and went back inside.

Mom put her big, knockoff Chanel sunglasses on and looked up. "Kind of ugly, huh?"

I read the informational plaques posted on the white fence. "Some white guy made these? And this is the symbol of the neighborhood?" I stared skeptically at the colorful glass fragments catching the sunlight.

Mom shrugged. "When the Watts riots happened, they left the towers alone. Everyone wants something to mark their neighborhood."

The Watts riots—Bobby had lived through them, and yet that history felt ancient, even more remote than Sa-i-gu. "America has some serious social amnesia," I said. "In all those news reports from 1992, the reporters are so shocked, like, *My god, here, in Los Angeles?*"

Mom clicked her tongue. "*We* warned people. Bobby and I were on a panel and some reporter asked if there could be another Watts riot. Bobby said, 'Like Watts, but worse.'" Mom fanned herself with her hand. "The reporter didn't like that."

"Now Ferguson and Baltimore are burning and people are surprised again."

"Like you said, you'd never even been to Watts. That's how people are: if the problem isn't right in front of them, they ignore it."

"But I made it a point to educate myself."

"Of course you did. Not everyone has the time or resources."

"So what, being an activist is itself a privilege?"

Mom lowered her gaze from the towers down to me. "You have a lot to learn, my son. Ready to go?"

I glanced back at the alien edifices. I'd come to embed myself in the history of this place, but instead I felt like a tourist. I had no idea how to close the distance between myself and the people I supposedly stood for.

We got back into the car and I backed out of the sleepy street. The seat belts and steering wheel were hot to the touch from those few minutes. Mom turned the AC on and a rush of air dissipated the heat.

Mom smacked her lips. "Why don't we get some water."

"Single-use plastics?"

"Ai. You want to stay thirsty?" Mom pointed out the window. "Here's a place."

I didn't have it in me to argue and swerved into the strip mall. A sign with classic black letters against a yellow background advertised STAR DELI in the corner.

We pushed through the door and an electronic eye dinged above us. I blinked to adjust to the dark interior. Mom strode back to the refrigeration units with drinks illuminated like gems. She chose a bottle and brought it to the register. A window of thick fiberglass protected the cashier and the easy-to-steal items: lottery cards, Advil, cigarettes, and condoms.

The man behind the counter rose slowly and turned to us. He was

Korean, naturally, with a square face dotted by liver spots. He wore a gray cargo vest, despite the heat outside, as if he were ready for a long journey or a battle.

Mom looked around the store. "I swear, this looks familiar."

The man rang up the water. "Two fifty," he said.

She handed him the money, then switched to Korean and said something about meetings.

He looked up, and his heavy-lidded eyes moved across my mother's face, as if deciding whether or not to acknowledge her.

I realized what Mom was asking and saw an opening. "Excuse me," I said. "Did you live through Sa-i-gu?"

He made an expression so cold it could almost pass for neutral. Mom repeated the question in Korean.

The man answered with a phlegmy, dismissive rasp from the back of his throat. He handed Mom her change.

"Hey," I said, "you could be a little friendlier, considering my mother tried to repair relations between you and the customers that gave you a livelihood."

The man gave me that cold stare again. Then, like something ignited inside him, he started to shout in Korean. He flung his arm out and then slammed his palm on the counter, speaking too quickly for me to understand. I froze, mesmerized by his scowling face. Mom motioned me outside.

We paused under the overhang in front of the store. It ensured, as with so many things in L.A., that the customer spent as little time exposed to the elements as possible. The asphalt lot steamed in the heat.

"What an asshole," said Mom in a jaded voice, unscrewing the cap. She drank and then turned to me. "How nice that my son is standing up for his mother." She reached over to tap my cheek and I stepped away.

"What was he saying?"

"Oh, you know—*those sons of bitches, I gave them jobs, and they still burned me out.* That kind of thing."

She handed me the bottle and I drank the cool, electrolyte-infused water. My throat was so dry the liquid almost hurt. I took another sip and felt my guts rumble as they processed the alcohol from last night.

"Cool, so he thinks people should be grateful for being exploited."

"Do you appreciate your mother's work now?" asked Mom. "Dealing with people like that all the time?"

"Why does anyone shop here, if he's like that?" I asked.

Mom chuckled. "You know, that was one of our campaigns during the Coalition. We handed out these etiquette guidelines, saying, *Smile at customers* and *Place the change in their hands, not on the counter.*" She shook her head. "My people."

"Rudeness is some inherently Korean thing?"

"Working fourteen-hour days and in a shitty store where you might be shot doesn't help."

"Oh, come on," I said. "That's just colonizer's paranoia—that you're going to be killed because you're not wanted there."

"They *were* being killed." Mom grunted. "Of course, that's not how the media told it, or how the history is written."

I shook my head as I worked to square this with what I knew. "Well, but the Black community was in a position of captivity, while Koreans were extracting resources to build their middle-class livelihoods elsewhere."

"Would you have said that to the parents whose seven-year-old daughter was shot in a robbery? To the widows of the men who were killed in their stores?" Mom let the question hover. "Koreans had this dilemma: Do we try to talk about the violence we're suffering and hold press conferences like the other side? Or do we just keep it quiet and hope it stops? Guess which they chose."

Over my shoulder I could just see into the deli and make out the back of the man's head through the register window. I understood that fiberglass wasn't just there to display cigarettes—it was bulletproof.

I'd started sweating again and felt drained. We got into the car, turned on the engine, and blasted the AC. I looked at the map on my phone and an idea came to me.

"We're right by Florence and Normandie!" I said.

"Whatever you want," said Mom. "It's your history lesson."

We were only ten minutes from the intersection where people first gathered that evening in April 1992, when all four cops who beat Rodney King bloody were let off with nothing. I'd rewatched the famous footage, preserved on YouTube: a news helicopter circled above the crowds milling in gas stations, throwing bottles and rocks at any car driven by a white person; some guys pulled a truck driver from his cab and kicked him in the ribs, the face. It was where that intangible shift happened, when the clink of breaking glass announced to the millions watching that the rules of everyday life were suspended, because the rules never were made for some.

We approached the intersection. "Good," said Mom. "I need to gas up. You know, this car is so fuel efficient I forget."

"Seriously? You're going to gas up at *those* stations?"

"So dramatic. Pull in."

I drove into the 76, which was, to be fair, like any in L.A. with its boxy white awning and a little booth in the center. It seemed wrong for it to lack any historical marker, any sign of what began there. But for that to happen, we'd have to live in a society that wanted to understand that history instead of writing it off as a mob of discontented Black and Brown people who wanted to smash windows and grab shoes.

Mom unscrewed the gas tank and swiped her card. I leaned on the car beside her, squinting against the heavy sun. The gasoline fumes pressed into my nose and mouth like a gag. We were far from the ocean, far from everything light and breezy that made the pop version of L.A.

Another gas station sat across the street, and the two other corners opened onto driveways for an auto parts store and a deli. This was L.A.'s makeshift town square, its piazza: two gas stations with enough open space for a few dozen people to come together and shout, *No justice, no peace.*

"Where were you that day?" I asked Mom.

She kept looking at the pump display as it ticked up the price. "Same place as everyone else: at home watching the shit go down on the news."

"You and Bobby didn't, like, do some emergency convening?"

Mom kept staring at the pump, as if it were easier to talk to it than me. "I tried. That night, there was a meeting at the First AME in South Central. Bobby and I took separate cars, but it was so crowded I had to circle and circle and finally ended up near some Korean deli. Even during a riot it was hard to park." She smiled weakly. "I got out of the car and started walking. Then I realized the people around me were stopping and staring: like, what the fuck is this Korean woman doing alone in South Central right now? But it wasn't curiosity. I'll never forget their eyes, the intensity. I realized I could die. I got back in and drove. That night, I saw the deli on the news, on fire."

I looked around this intersection again. It seemed impossible that anyone would wish us harm, would find our Asian faces anything but unusual. "Didn't that kind of run counter to the Coalition? Wasn't the point to show up?"

"And what," said Mom, turning to me and raising her voice, "get the crap beaten out of me? You know what happened to people that day?"

"Okay, okay." I changed course. "I guess what I'm saying is, how did the Coalition work with all the anti-Black violence during the uprising? I mean, the whole reason Koreans were targeted, right, was because of Soon Ja Du killing Latasha Harlins over a bottle of orange juice."

Mom's lips thinned. "It's a little more complicated than that."

"How? It was on tape." We'd watched the famous fuzzy gray security footage in preparation for a teach-in and I remember Tiff and Ash grunting in disgust. "Harlins was walking away when Du slammed a bullet into the back of her head."

"They edited that tape," said Mom. "The two of them were in a big fight right before, swinging at each other and throwing things."

"Mom, do you hear yourself? Du was a forty-year-old woman with a gun, and Harlins was fifteen."

"Obviously I'm not saying it was justified," said Mom through a clenched jaw. "I feel for that girl and her family—it was terrible. But Du was probably this traumatized woman who didn't know the country or language and was on edge from working nonstop, and she panicked."

"Right, just like Liang 'panicked' in the stairwell." Frustration rose in me. "In each case, one person had a gun and wasn't dead at the end. One was innocent because of being Asian and one was guilty for being Black. They 'didn't mean it,' and anyway they kind of look like us, so we should forgive them and move on." I paused for breath. "You guys condemned the killing, right? The Coalition."

"It's not that simple. Like I said, I was working for the city—we couldn't take sides."

"*Take sides*? What other side is there to take?"

"Of course we said that the killing was a tragedy. But we couldn't say, *Du was a murderer*. Or *Boycott Du's store*, like the people picketing. That would've alienated the Korean side of the Coalition."

"God forbid they lose a little business."

"Not 'a little business,'" Mom said sharply. "This was their livelihood."

"If the Coalition couldn't say something as simple as that, what was the point?" I knew this was harsh but momentum pushed me forward, and I wanted to see how far it would take me.

"You don't understand how it was then," Mom shot back. "It was intense. We were getting shit on all sides. We even got death threats."

"So what?" I cut her off. "We're getting death threats!" I liked saying it, the power of it. "That doesn't stop us: all it means is that we're moving people. We have those conservative Chinese scared."

The gas pump clicked off with a shudder. The nozzle sat silent and lifeless in the tank.

"What?" said Mom. Her voice thinned.

"So what," I repeated. "Some friend sent me a link to some right-wing message boards posting my photo and calling me names."

"Reed—I told you not to be on that Twitter thing. How did they get your photo?"

"You don't know what you're talking about. This isn't Twitter, these are shadow forums—people are such cowards that they want to stay anonymous."

"Cowards are *more* dangerous!" she pleaded. "You could get hurt."

The concern in Mom's voice made me furious. I looked above and behind her. "I'm not even getting the worst of it. They found Tiff's address and posted it, with rape and death threats. But who the fuck are we going to report it to, the cops?" I took a breath. "People are *dying*. Cops are hunting Black folks, and Asian people are ready to condone it if it means getting a taste of whiteness."

"Reed," Mom steadied herself and her words came out smooth, like steel. "This is not your crisis. I want you to stop. I'm serious."

I snorted. "*That's* your take? Only work on a crisis if you can do it safely? Some organizer you've become."

Mom's eyes flashed and her hand shot toward me, cutting the space between us. It moved from pure instinct, a bird darting through the air.

The hand froze. It stood, suspended, as if realizing what it was doing. I looked in Mom's eyes and they were no longer pleading or angry but watery with confusion. The hand lowered slowly, as if by pulley.

But it had been there, inches away. Both of us saw it and saw each other seeing it. And even though it hadn't made contact it summoned a monstrous force—some leviathan had surfaced from just below our conversations, even if just to show us its barbed spine.

I got inside the car and slammed the door. A low ringing came into my ears. I willed myself to believe that I'd won, that I'd stood against Mom's failure to take a stance.

Mom slid into the driver's seat quietly and started the car. A hard silence held us. "I'm sorry, Reed. Okay?" said Mom. "I stopped myself, didn't I?"

I gritted my teeth and let anger seethe in me. The sense of victory would slip away if I accepted her apology. I forced myself to stare forward as we passed the cheap, faded signs of South Central, each block reminding me why people wanted to set the whole thing on fire.

"Listen," she said in a tired voice. "I don't know what you're trying to prove. If you need me to say you're a better organizer than me—fine. You're smarter, you're more focused than I was at your age. You have a stronger analysis. I can say all this, but I don't think it's going to make you happy."

A silent, horrible scream filled my brain, rejecting all those admissions I'd supposedly wanted. I should've gloated, but I only wanted to cry. I clenched my throat instead.

To cede even an inch would mean admitting that Mom wasn't in control at that moment, admitting that she was driven by a power that I knew even though I couldn't name or understand it, a power that was consuming me even in that moment.

"Who said anything about being happy?" I muttered.

Mom recoiled, as if I'd tried to hit her back. She pulled onto the freeway and we shot forward, the flat city blurring below us.

XIII

I ROLLED OPEN THE DOOR OF THE garage. It sat unused behind our home and now served the same function it had throughout high school: a place for me to be away from Mom.

The overhead light offered a murky yellow to the big room. Everything sat in a settled chaos, shoved away in a hurry and then forgotten for years: an upturned table hugged the wall, picture frames leaned against each other like dominoes.

One corner was dedicated to my stuff, which Mom had stored after I left for college: the electric guitar I'd begged for in high school collected dust in its elegant curves, cardboard boxes marked REED formed a small pyramid. I opened the one on top and saw it was filled with my old paperbacks: *The Unbearable Lightness of Being*, *The Stranger*, a handful of Murakamis—the heavy philosophical shit CJ and I discussed over boba, beginning, in our clumsy, not-yet-Ivy-League way, to amass cultural capital.

I felt like an archaeologist reconstructing the life of an eighteen-year-old, the one who'd used that trite "be the change you want to see" Gandhi quotation in his college essay; an eighteen-year-old who couldn't wait to vote for Obama that fall, who would check *Politico* and spout off on bills moving in the House, who went to high school debate just to argue with moral superiority against the Orange County kids about the death penalty and gay marriage.

Of course I swung to the other extreme, embarrassed by that naive faith in American democracy. I wanted to pretend I'd never been the freshman who threw away the Band-Aid Tiff handed him, who always understood policing, who had never been anti-Black in any way. So I desperately buried that self, shoveling so much analysis over it that the grave became a conspicuous mound.

Dad cleared his throat behind me. He looked small in the big mouth of the garage and blinked inquiringly through his glasses. "You and Mom haven't had one of your . . . upsets in a few years," he said. He came over and peered into the open box. "Back in the day," he continued, "we called that a denouncement. You had to struggle with your parents' bourgeois tendencies."

"We have the Marxist-Leninist weapon of criticism and self-criticism," I said, quoting Mao.

"Right," he said. "Unfortunately, turns out it's hard to build a movement when you keep ejecting people for not being perfect."

Dad shoved a box to the side, revealing an imposing set of hardcover blue books. "Since you're so into our pasts, maybe you'll want these." Gold letters etched into the spines read *The Works of V. I. Lenin.* The tomes were authoritative and alluring, promising a young revolutionary the accumulated knowledge of one of the few people who actually did the thing—had the analysis and statesmanship and timing to change the world one October a hundred years ago. Never mind how it turned out.

But a fatigue came over me just looking at the volumes, and I knew there was no way I'd read them. I'd never be a good communist. I'd have to be a good something else.

"You read all of those?"

Dad laughed. "Never. It was a wedding gift from one of our movement friends."

"At least it's better than a food processor."

He shrugged. "I would've used a food processor." He picked up a metal folding chair off the wall, wiped off the dust, and tried to look natural as he placed himself in it. He took off his glasses, which made him look blank and doughy, all the structure gone from his face. This meant Dad was about to say something serious, as if by not seeing the world as clearly, he could bear it better. "Have you ever googled us?"

I cocked my head. "Why would I do that?"

"You've never been curious what they say about us out there?"

I pulled out my phone and typed his name into the search bar. Even though it was the most public, obvious way to find out information about him, it felt sneaky, as if the person in front of me was not who he said.

The first link was his employee profile at the union; the second was an *L.A. Times* article quoting him about the minimum wage increase. I clicked on the third, which brought me to a wiki-style page. I did a quick scroll: it was a detailed article, the length a semifamous actor's would be. It had photographs, a timeline of his organizing work, and a record of his trips to China. I scrolled back to the top and saw the tagline for the website: "Uncovering the Globalist Influence in American Politics."

My head popped up. "What the hell is this?"

"Someone already did your movement history for you," he joked drily.

I read back through and it did, indeed, talk about his communist days, with blue links to Mom and a dozen of their friends—people I knew from dinners and parties at our house. There were records of fundraisers they'd attended, conferences where they'd spoken.

"This is nuts," I said. "Who's doing this?"

Dad shrugged. "Some right-wing crazies with too much time and money. Keep going."

I went back to the search results. The next link was another site that ranked leftist public figures in L.A., with a meter that ranked him with four and a half out of five raised fists. A few links down was a fringe news site that had taken a clip of Dad speaking at a rally and tied it to his communist past.

Dad managed a half smile. "Not bad for your aging, moderate old man, huh?"

"You're proving your lefty cred?"

He exhaled through his nose. "Mom told me about the threats."

I avoided Dad's worried eyes.

"It took me a long time to learn this, Reed, but these little threats, these fringe radicals—they're very organized."

"So what?" I snapped. "You're unpopular with some conservatives?"

"It's more than that. Did you know your grandfather always wanted me to be a politician?" Dad's confident, rhetorical voice dropped away and he became a private person, almost shy. "He had it in his head: *L.A.'s first Chinese mayor.* Or *the congressman from Chinatown.* I never took it seriously, except once. I'd just joined the union and run a successful back-wages campaign. They were looking for some fresh blood to oust this old, corrupt city councilor who'd been there forever. And so this union boss called me in and asked if I'd thought about running. I said I'd give it a shot, and he told me that was great, and I'd be getting a call from the DNC. The DNC never called. The next time I saw the boss he avoided me, and I understood: they'd looked into my past and knew I'd be red-baited the moment I ran."

I squeezed my eyes closed. As much as Dad's unflappable confidence annoyed me, I didn't want to hear this from him, didn't want to think of him as vulnerable, as an idealistic young person confronting the limits of what he could do.

"It was hard to explain that one to your grandfather." Dad shrugged. "Who knows, I might've lost. I always hated fundraising. But this is what those right-wingers want: they want to take away our options, want to paint us as Reds to delegitimize us. Back then, they probably had to hire someone to find all these old articles and research my past. Now it only takes one Google search, and just like that, all these doors shut.

"All our friends—the ones linked to on the site—any time one of them gets a public appointment or lands a new job we all take this breath of relief. We've lived with this long, long shadow. And the terrible thing is, you don't know where it's coming from or how much of it is in your head."

I pressed my palms against my eyes. American meritocracy was a scam, sure; and I knew our police state bugged everyone from Dr. King to librarians, but I'd never understood how well it worked, how it had become so ingrained in the culture that the government didn't even have to do the work.

I snapped my eyes open. "Well, what then?" I demanded. "We just stop organizing so that we can secure our professional jobs and rise through this shitty system—maybe become president of it one day?"

Dad's face went weary, as if he were disappointed in my argument. "Of course not, Reed. I never said that. I'm only trying to show you how deep these systems go, how effective they are."

"I swear, if this is going to be about *compromise*—"

"No one said that, either. You can keep going exactly like you are, and that's fine—that's what Mom and I did. We didn't know about COINTEL-PRO back then, or the extent of the surveillance, but we definitely knew we were being watched. I don't regret anything. The only difference now is that we've seen what this country did to our friends who weren't as lucky—who didn't have, as you say, the same privilege. So we want you to understand the choices you're making. And there are ways to do it that are smarter, aren't so confrontational, and are no less radical or effective."

"Sounds nice," I said petulantly.

"You're smart enough to know the difference between performing politics and living them."

"That's not how it is anymore," I said. "How you show up in the world is also how you change it. How you talk about the movement *is* the movement."

I could tell Dad believed me, had seen this in the young people he worked with, and that he was at a loss. "That sounds very difficult."

I shrugged, feeling another hollow point scored. I was tired of my way of being right.

Dad sighed. "You wanted our organizing lessons, and this is what we learned, what we have to offer. Because if you don't know, it's like Marx said: the first time is tragedy—"

"I know," I cut him off. "The second, farce."

XIV

THE CAVERNOUS STATION AT WIL-
shire and Western was empty, and I sat alone on a cement bench. Part of
the joke known as the L.A. Metro was that, because it was mostly useless,
it felt clean and new. I refreshed Twitter looking for new posts about the
march, then swiped off my phone to save the dying battery. The train
glided into the station without the awful clatter I'd grown used to in New
York. I stepped inside and saw the seats were optimistically covered in
fabric. I'd worn my T-shirt with BLACK LIVES MATTER in bold white
letters against a dark blue, and enjoyed the mix of nervous looks and
meaningful eye contact with the handful of other passengers.

I couldn't stay home, I couldn't call CJ to hang out. I had no story of
Black-Asian solidarity to take with me, no strategies from the past generation to show us the way. Marching was the one thing I knew, a way to
put my body on the line.

I emerged at Pershing Square, a rare attempt at public space. I had
to circle the square twice, with its bad sight lines and awkward low-rise
steps, to find the cluster of a few dozen protesters gathered below an arch.

Someone saw me and handed me a piece of cardboard that read END

POLICE BRUTALITY. I felt the familiar comfort of the protest: to walk into the crowd a total stranger and merge into a collective body where all of us knew what to do.

The smallness of the rally felt edgy. I didn't see anyone securing a perimeter or communicating with walkie-talkies; no National Lawyers Guild observers in neon yellow hats. A few of the protesters were anarchists in black with bandanas over their faces. One of them shook out his limbs like a boxer before a spar.

I stepped back from the crowd and snapped a photo and posted it on Twitter, writing that L.A. was in solidarity with the protests in New York. I added a line about killer cops, then thought about Dad, and how this tweet was undoubtedly being stored in some NSA computer, and deleted it.

A Black woman, maybe forty, with the no-bullshit air of a teacher, stepped onto a concrete divider and held out her arms for balance. "Tonight we want to send some love to the family of Akai Gurley," she yelled. "Tonight we say that the criminal justice system that let off his killer is the same one killing our brothers and sisters here."

The crowd cheered and we began to move through old downtown. It was a ghost city at night, with shuttered businesses and homeless camps zipped up. Our chant of *What do we want? Justice!* echoed through the empty streets.

The group of anarchists had its own chants. Someone yelled *Hands up!* and the rest threw finger pistols in the air and screamed *Shoot back!* A ripple of discomfort moved through the rest of the crowd—we didn't want to join their chant but couldn't get rid of them.

The anarchists formed a line and stopped traffic so that we could move off the sidewalk into the street. Car horns blasted: some rhythmic beeps supporting us, others blaring at us to get off the road. The impatient ones changed lanes to swerve around. It was thrilling to march in the street, to assert ourselves in this city where cars ruled.

We came to a red light. The crowd waited tensely, clapping to keep up the rhythm of the march. One of the anarchists broke away and stood on a car hood. I reached for my phone and started recording, even though my battery was dying. One thing we'd learned: it was always better to have a video.

"No!" the woman who was leading us yelled at him. "Do *not* fuck with property."

"Fuck property!" the man yelled. He'd cut the sleeves off his black hoodie to show his muscles, which glowed under the streetlights like eggshells. "And fuck these people." He shot an arm out and we followed his pointing finger to one of the new restaurants gentrifying downtown— the kind of restaurant Mom would want to try. "Bring the fight where it hurts."

The floor-to-ceiling windows, illuminated by chic, neon curlicues showed a crowd of diners, all white and Asian. The couple closest to the street turned to look at us, and the man gave a smarmy smile that said he was totally down with the cause but no, he would not be interrupting his clams to do anything about it.

The anarchists began chanting: *Shut. It. Down.* The man atop the car pumped a fist, screaming to match everyone else. *Shut. It. Down.* I scanned the crowd. Half were deep in the chant, bulls staring at the red flag of the restaurant. The streetlights seemed to grow brighter, the cool air in my nose sharper. I locked eyes with one of my neighbors, each of us silently asking if this was happening.

"NO!" the woman yelled again, so strongly that the chant paused. "Do *not* go in there!" she screamed. "That's how they *arrest us*." The man let his arms drop and the collective body stopped, tense with indecision.

A car horn ripped through the silence. The driver leaned on it, the head-splitting blast a crude reminder of how much louder than us it could be. The traffic light had turned green. Another car joined in, making it punishing for us to stand there. The horns flooded the air, dissonant, bouncing across the canyon of buildings and into the blotchy purple sky.

The anarchists peeled off and followed the man into the restaurant, like pollen separating from a dandelion. "NO!" the woman yelled again, this time with the frustration and panic of an older sister.

Shut. It. Down! The anarchists chanted as they moved into the restaurant, and the man by the window tried to hide his horror behind a mask of cool. A few diners took out their phones to record and show their scandalized friends later, or maybe to share with the cops.

"Keep moving!" the woman said, now leading the twenty of us left. We clung closer together, pressed between the parked cars and those slowing and dodging around us.

A flitter of red and blue light dashed across the buildings, then came the terrible, mechanical *whoop* of a cop car.

"Stay together!" the leader yelled.

Mom's advice flashed in my head. I was sixteen and she was driving me to one of my first protests, against the anti-immigrant bill in the House. As I got out of the car, her face went stony and she said, *If it gets out of hand with the cops, always run with the crowd.* I asked her why. *If they catch you alone they'll beat the crap out of you.* It took me all these years to understand how she knew that.

The cops whooped again. They were getting closer.

"Stay together!" Panic splintered the leader's voice and I felt adrenaline surging through me, readying my limbs for danger.

The protesters began running. They scattered forward and to the sides. I flung my sign to the ground and bolted, tearing across the cement.

The police whooped and a voice through the car megaphone told us, in a bored voice, not to run. I cut to the left and came to a deserted street. I'd never known my way around downtown and its maze of one-way streets. Even here, people didn't walk if they could help it.

I turned right, came to another quiet street, and paused. A tent encampment leaned against a chain link fence and a lone car sped by. No one would know there was a protest going on a few blocks away, that a dozen people led by some white anarchist were yelling in the faces of wealthy diners or probably, by this point, being handcuffed.

My heart thumped but I knew I had some time and took out my phone. An empty white battery flashed on my screen, scolding me for not keeping it charged.

I ran across the street to a 7-Eleven, its neon lights creating a surreal oasis in the dark. I stepped inside and squinted. A South Asian man, his eyes rimmed with red from exhaustion, sat behind the counter—eyes that flashed open when I came in.

"Hey," I gasped, out of breath. "Any chance you have a charger I could use? For like, five minutes?"

The man stood up, emanating a mix of alarm and outrage. "No trouble," he said. He swung his arms like an umpire calling safe.

"No, no," I said. I took out my phone and showed him the dead battery symbol.

The man was staring at my T-shirt, where BLACK LIVES MATTER glowed like evidence under the bloodless light. I was sweating, too, and probably looked crazed from the running.

"You see?" he grunted impatiently. He pointed across the store, where, above the magazine rack, an ugly slice of plywood had taken the place of a window. "You people. Last week."

"That wasn't me," I said, raising my voice back but embarrassed by the childishness of my retort.

"You running from the police? Causing trouble? I'll call them."

He took out his phone, and suddenly we were in a silly standoff, each of us holding our little gadgets, one as a request and one as a threat. So much for our supposed "community."

"It's because of Asians like you that we're in this fucking mess," I said, my chest thudding. "Call the cops. But when shit really goes down, see if they come help *you*."

My anger wasn't spent yet. I looked around and saw a turnstile display of phone chargers and cords beside the counter, as if mocking me, as if saying, *If only you hadn't worn that shirt, or had been able to keep your cool, you could've bought one of these for $8.99 and been home in twenty minutes.*

I lunged forward and shoved the turnstile, sending the flimsy tower careening. It crashed with a pathetic, anticlimactic shudder, a few vacuum-sealed cords scattering across the floor.

"Son of a bitch!" the man roared.

But I was already pushing through the door, sprinting so hard that my lungs ached and my feet throbbed from impact. I ran until I was out of sight again, on some other nondescript downtown block and, I understood, totally screwed. The man was probably calling the cops and there were a dozen cars within a few blocks, picking off protesters one by one, just like Mom warned. And there was, in all likelihood, exactly one East Asian male walking around downtown L.A. with a Black Lives Matter shirt. Fear rose through me in waves of cold and hot. I heaved a breath, and a needle of clarity jabbed me—I knew what to do.

I ducked behind a bus bench, scanned the empty street, and peeled off my T-shirt. The sweat made it sticky and I shuddered as the night air hit my bare torso. I turned the shirt inside out, gave it a shake, ripped off the tag on the neck, and put it back on. Now I was just an Asian kid. I was no one. I saw with revolting clarity how easy it was to cover the one thing that marked me as a target, because it was not my skin.

I began walking, slowly, and anyone paying attention would've laughed at my studied casualness, the way I fought my impulse to sprint. I regulated my breath and willed myself not to look around. A cop car, siren on, came up behind me. I continued my imitation of a pedestrian, even looking at my dead phone. The siren's whine rose in pitch, then it charged straight past me, the pitch declining.

I stopped and heaved another breath, resting my arms on my knees. I probably could have wiped my face and gone up to ask the cop for directions.

I kept walking until I came across one of those gray, boxy relics from my childhood. It made sense that in downtown, with its homeless and precarious, with its immigrant poor who couldn't buy a several-hundred-dollar pocket computer, there would still be a pay phone or two left. I picked up the black chunk of plastic and I held it to my face. It smelled like vinegar. The letters of the pad were worn away, but I could still make out enough to spell COLLECT.

It rang with analog fuzz. The line clicked alive and I didn't have to ask who it was.

"Mom," I said. I almost retched. I wanted anything but to say that horrible cliché, the pathetic return to teenhood: "I need you to pick me up."

* * *

Streetlights swiped across Mom's face as she drove. We rolled quietly through the empty city. It felt dreamy under the cloudy sky, as if all this concrete and asphalt and cinderblock were immaterial. I glanced over for a hint at her thoughts and found nothing except lines drawn under her eyes from exhaustion.

"Why didn't you run with the crowd?" she said at last. Her voice had lost all its emotion; she was an interviewer going through rote questions.

"Everyone dispersed," I said. I described the scene in front of the restaurant.

"How many people were at this rally?"

"Maybe thirty."

"My son," she said, "you join a small, poorly organized rally, you forget to charge your phone, and then you get separated from the crowd? What happened to the trained activist?"

"Fine." The sweat on my skin was turning clammy, and I felt the Black Lives Matter lettering glomming to my chest, reminding me that I'd betrayed it. "I'm full of shit," I said. I lifted up my T-shirt and showed her the lettering and explained how I hid. "You're right," I explained. "I talk a lot, I have a lot of theories. And when it came down to it, all I could think was to run and hide."

"I'm not happy you went to the protest," she said. "But I'm glad you did that."

My eyes burned with irritation. "Why."

"Because I care about you, my son. And it's just not worth it."

The irritation flooded through my head and down my throat. I grimaced to hold it back.

"The mothers," said Mom, as if to cut me off. "The mothers of all those boys killed by the police. Do you ever think about them? How they'd give anything if all their sons had to do was flip a T-shirt inside out to be safe? Don't be so self-centered, Reed. There are times to fight and there are times to get home."

My chest constricted. I thought I was ready to face anything, but I never wanted to look right at its center, where Mom was pointing—at the story of every mother and family tied to those names we chanted. I was an emotional coward. I wanted justice for them, yes, but not to touch their suffering, afraid of what I might have to feel. And what kind of solidarity was that?

I thought of the night Eric Garner's killer walked without an indictment. A few thousand of us gathered at Atlantic-Pacific. A line of protesters in the front carried black caskets with the names of those killed by cops, and the families marched beside them. I found some organizers I knew from CAAAV and one handed me a sign that said BLACK LIVES MATTER in Chinese. I felt proud to hold it even though I couldn't read it.

We reached the foot of the Brooklyn Bridge and the energy changed. The protest swelled with the sound of clackers and whoops and chants. A group of kids jumped onto the concrete dividers and flung their hands in the air as if conducting the cascade of car horns on either side. The crowd took up Assata Shakur's chant: *It is our duty to fight for our freedom.* But surrounding the noise of our drums and clapping was a profound silence, and I looked to the side and saw the slow, dark churn of water. We were crawling along a strip of metal and asphalt, stories above a swirling, indifferent East River and under a black sky outlined by the two cables swooping between the stone towers of the bridge. We were immense—*It is our duty to win*—and microscopic. It felt, though I'd never believed in such a thing until then, sacred. *We must love and support each other,* we chanted, because the system would kill you and blame you for your death. So we had to be there, on that bridge, if for nothing than to show each other that every lost life demands we pause the world for a moment. *We have nothing to lose but our chains.*

It was the first time I glimpsed the truth that was now so clear: we gathered not just to make demands, not just to overturn the system, but because we needed to grieve together.

Mom pulled up in front of our house and cut the engine and sat still. They'd recently replaced the sulfur street lamps with LEDs, which lit up the street with empty white haloes. She stared forward like she wished there were more road ahead.

"Halmoni died," she said.

"Jesus," I said, then closed my jaw. "I mean, I'm sorry. When?"

"A few hours ago. I tried calling you, but."

"Sorry," I said, feeling silly and stumped for words. I glanced over and understood the weariness in Mom's face. Then I noticed her absence of expression and my own lack of tears, which had come so easily when Dad's parents died.

"There's not going to be a big funeral or anything," she said. "Halmoni had no friends."

"Mom."

She shrugged, unfazed. "It's true. Get some rest."

"But," I stammered. "How do you feel?"

Mom let her eyes close and released a slow exhale. "I don't know."

XV

A GOLDEN BUDDHA FLANKED BY two attendants gazed over the living room from the space where most people would put a TV. Mom, Dad, and I stood in our socks on the straw floor watching the abbess bow to the buddha while an ahjuma in a pink puffer struck a bulbous wooden instrument with a mallet.

The recommendation for this abbess came, of course, through one of Mom's friends, who assured us that unlike some of the fancier temples in K-Town, this one wasn't grubbing for donations. The temple was a brown single-family home on the edge of K-Town with a driveway. The living room was divided into the altar, where we stood, and the dining room of a middle-aged Korean woman, with its baroque wood furniture covered in doilies.

Mom soaked in the ceremony. Dad shifted his weight and glanced around the room, then shifted his weight again. In fifth grade, I'd had to ask my parents what their religion was. Dad answered, without hesitation, "Atheist." Mom told me to check *Other* and write in *Spiritual*, to which Dad guffawed. It made sense now, given how the two shifted out of their communist days: Dad's materialist pragmatism, Mom's turn toward the holistic.

The abbess stood and turned to us. Her head was shaved, which forced my eyes onto her slight, impish smile, sharpened by a long jaw. She motioned for us to come over to the altar, where we'd placed a fruit basket and three platters of rice cakes. A framed photograph of Halmoni, cropped so that she was alone, stood between two candles. It was maybe fifteen years old and one of the few in which she seemed happy.

The abbess lit an incense stick that unraveled in a slow curlicue of smoke and offered a sweet, woody smell. She bowed, picked up a cup of water on the altar, and swirled it three times over the altar. She put it down and gestured for Mom to do the same. Mom knelt and picked up the cup. The abbess cleared her throat. Mom blinked in embarrassment, stood up, placed her palms together, and bowed to the buddha before kneeling. The abbess grinned and gave a thumbs-up, then gestured for me to follow.

I made eye contact with Dad but he looked as lost as me. I gave an awkward bow, then knelt. My knees crashed into the mat with a little ripple of pain. I stared at Halmoni's image. My hands trembled as I moved the cup over the incense. I was afraid to do this wrong, this ritual I'd never seen or heard of but that suddenly felt endowed with significance. I finally had a chance to do something for Halmoni, even though she wasn't Buddhist or Christian but believed most of all in money.

I got up, and the abbess, sensing Dad's hesitation, gestured him forward with both hands. Dad jerked through an abrupt bow, knelt, and swerved the cup around quickly, like he was afraid to touch it for too long. He rocked back up and stood by us, face flushed.

"Good ja!" The abbess said, and gave us a little clap. She closed her eyes, sang something slow and primordial, then turned and gestured us over to the dining table. The ahjuma came over with one of the platters of rice cakes.

"Have some," said Mom. "Dinner's not for a little while."

I looked down at the green and white balls, stacked in piles of concentric circles. "Aren't these for, like, Halmoni's spirit?"

"When did you get so religious?" Mom said, as she picked out an assortment. "We paid for them."

I looked over to the abbess, who was sitting in the corner cross-legged, already popping a rice cake into her mouth.

Dad and I exchanged glances, then each took a few. The room was silent except for our mouths smacking against the sticky things.

The ahjuma came by and served us some pale, yellow tea. I took a sip. It was bitter and complemented the sweet cakes. The snack felt Korean and ancient, and I found this comforting, like maybe this was something Halmoni would've known.

The abbess stood up and disappeared behind a doorway at the other end of the room. I chewed my fourth rice cake as the ahjuma gestured for Mom to follow.

"Be right back," said Mom.

Dad and I sat there like lost children, both of us chewing slowly so that we'd have something to do.

"It's a good thing nothing broke," he said finally, clearing his throat. "At the 7-Eleven. The man probably won't press charges and it's not worth their time to make an arrest."

I nodded and kept chewing through the awkward quiet.

"When I was arrested, your grandfather had to pick me up from the station," said Dad.

I paused and the rice cake jammed against my palate. I waited for him to go on.

"One of our 'strategies' back then was graffiti. *Down with the capitalist system*, things like that. We were desperate." Dad spoke quickly, rushing out the words. "Your grandfather never looked as mortified as he did that night in the station—it was unimaginable for his generation. But he posted bail and drove me home. That's when I learned what it is to be a parent. To be someone's child."

I sipped my tea and tried to integrate this mild, middle-aged person next to me with the young radical so frustrated and desperate that he spray-painted the city.

"Your grandmother, on the other hand, bought us rubber gloves so we wouldn't get paint on our hands," said Dad, misty-eyed. "There really are communist sympathizers everywhere," he said to cut the seriousness.

Mom emerged from the room. Her eyes had that fresh, tender gleam from crying. She sat back down without looking at either of us and drank her tea.

The ahjuma poked her head into the room and gestured for me. I hesitated. I didn't want to interrupt Mom's moment to ask her what this was about. I got up and followed the woman through the door, which led to a vestibule. The ahjuma pointed to another door, and I stepped through into a room lit by a few candles. The abbess sat on a cushion in the middle of the room, and behind her was another buddha.

I sat on the cushion facing her and folded my legs in front of me, wondering if I was doing it in the proper way. The abbess was the same person as before, with the same sly smile, but in the candlelight and the darkness she appeared very still, as if she'd become a statue, too.

"Uh," I said, "what is this?"

The abbess let out a low, raspy chuckle. "Your mother's idea."

I snorted. What else was new.

"Lots of pain," she said. She grimaced and pointed to her head.

Pain. In my head. I supposed it was true. "Yeah. What do I do about that?"

"Come back here." She pointed to her heart. "At first, more pain. Then less, less."

I wanted to say no thanks, more pain was not so interesting to me right now, was actually the last thing I needed after condescending to everyone I cared about only for my hypocrisy to explode in my face. I placed a hand on my heart anyway. My thoughts trailed off as I became absorbed by the low, welling ache there, an oceanic force. I released my hand.

"Ouch," I said.

"Heh, heh," said the abbess. "Good ja." She gave me a thumbs-up.

I laughed, disarmed. Suddenly I admired this person before me, who was somehow both an elder and a child.

"Here," she pointed to my head, "harsh, judge, limited. Here," she pointed to my heart, "everything allowed."

She bowed to me and I bowed back. I stood up and floated back through the vestibule into the living room.

Mom and Dad were sitting, talking softly to each other. They stopped when I came in and Mom turned to me questioningly. I shrugged.

The abbess walked in and clapped her hands. All of us jumped up like trained animals.

Mom reached into her Goyard purse and pulled out a white envelope. The abbess brushed it away, as if it were a silly detail, and the ahjuma pointed to a wooden box with a slit by the door. Mom slipped the envelope in, then put on her sunglasses. She bowed to the abbess, which triggered a series of bows—the abbess bowed to us and Dad and I offered our clumsy bows back. The ahjuma joined in, too, starting a second round.

The abbess came outside with us. I turned to her, just as I was stepping off the porch, and said, "Thank you." It came out as an awkward half shout. "Really."

"Heh, heh." She grinned and tapped her heart. "Come back."

* * *

I sat in the back seat staring at the back of Mom's and Dad's heads. I wondered how many thousands of hours I'd passed this way, all the rush hours and road trips we'd spent in this little triangle. Mom and I still hadn't spoken about our fight and it had congealed into an uneasy weight between us. But we were in that odd emotional space that opened up after a funeral, and I saw the opportunity to ask the obvious question.

"What did Halmoni think when you dropped out?"

My parents stiffened and I could feel the silent calculation pinging between them and Dad deferring to Mom's judgment.

"She disowned me," said Mom, without turning around.

A laugh escaped me. "Come on," I said. "Like in the K-dramas?"

Mom's face was a slab. "No. There was nothing dramatic about it. She just stopped talking to me. Wouldn't pick up the phone. I think she even wrote me out of her will. Not that she had any money," she added.

"Jesus," I sighed. I kept wanting to weigh Halmoni on that scale of good or bad, but every new detail about her rocked the levers, making it impossible to balance.

"Half the reason she came to America was because school was free, and she would've never been able to afford it for us in Korea," said Mom. "She even moved us into a better district for high school, though it was far from K-Town and harder for her to get around." Mom exhaled angrily, as if resenting what she had to say next. "I looked down on education and all that bourgeois stuff when we were in the movement—I didn't ask her for all that parental sacrifice bullshit. And for Halmoni it was always self-interest: if I got a good job, I could support her. But even with all that, she was doing the best she could as a mother. It took me a long time to admit that, because I wanted to stay angry."

"No offense?" I said. "You still seem angry."

Dad let out a guilty chuckle.

"Very funny," said Mom. "You were the reason we reconciled, you know. She wasn't willing to keep up the feud, not with a grandson."

Dad twisted his head to look at me. "Halmoni loved caring for you when you were a baby," he said, wanting to shift the tone. "I think those were some of her happiest years."

"She wiped your butt the way others polish jewelry," added Mom. "All of a sudden she was this kind, generous person. I was shocked, but I'm glad I got to see her that way at least once."

"I don't remember any of that," I said. A swelling filled my chest, constricting my lungs. "So I was a stinky baby, and you fulfilled the Confucian mandate to have boys."

"Aigul," said Mom. "It's not about that. You smiled and babbled and never lacked anything. So when she looked at you, she didn't feel she'd failed. Get it?"

XVI

I SAT AT THE MULHOLLAND DRIVE outlook leaning against the Prius and hugging my old bomber jacket around me against the night chill—my "heavy" jacket in high school, when I thought sixty degrees was frigid and anything below that uninhabitable. A layer of smog and mist settled over the basin, and the streetlights pulsed like glitching stars. I stared, waiting for anything else the city had to teach me. I'd wanted to fill myself with histories and instead felt like they'd been carved out of me.

My phone dinged. CJ ignored the long apology I had sent her and wrote instead:

Did I freaking kick you the other night?

Yeah you did

But I was being a dick

Fuck I need to stop drinking

Me too

But how else do we self-medicate under late capitalism?

Duh—pick me up in a bit

A tingle ran through me and it felt like my insides were smiling. I'd never been so eager to apologize. I'd been flayed of all my pretensions, all my grand ideas of myself, which suddenly made knowing what to do simple.

I got back into the Prius, turned on the overhead light, and took out my phone to FaceTime Tiff. It was late but I knew they'd be up. The phone rang a few beats and their face appeared.

"Hey," they said warily. Even over the small screen I could see they hadn't been sleeping. Their buzz cut had grown out and bluish circles ringed their eyes.

"So I've been having these conversations with my mom," I blurted, overriding the part of me that didn't want to say what I knew I had to. "I wanted to organize a teach-in or toolkit, to fill in our solidarity timeline. But I kept failing and failing and I realize it's because I was missing the deeper lesson: what it means to really know myself, ourselves. And to let that guide me. Anyway, I'm still committed to Black Lives Matter. I'll still show up for other rallies. But I can't get behind asking for Liang to go to jail."

Tiff sighed as if this were expected, as if it were a matter of time before I let them down. "We need Asian Americans to show up right now. But yeah, I understand: folks have to do what's right for them."

I shut my eyes. Tiff was talking to me as if I were a stranger, and I realized I'd felt this way a few times before but never had the courage to admit it to myself, let alone Tiff.

"I'm not 'Asian Americans,'" I said. "I'm not '*folks*.'"

Tiff's face changed, like they'd been stirred awake. Now they stared into the camera with focus.

"You're upset with me, okay," I pressed. "But talk to me like a person."

"Fine," they said. "I'm confused. A week ago you were ready to drop out of college to work on this case and now you don't even agree with the ask, right when we're trying to escalate. What the hell?"

I felt, to my surprise, totally stable, as if rooted into the mountain. "You know, we always talk about cross-generational dialogue, about learning from activists in the past. But here's the thing: you either extract a story that reinforces your beliefs, or you let that history change you. That's what happened. And I think our approach right now is going to burn us for a long time."

Tiff's face went slack, and the camera tilted up as if they'd forgotten they were holding it. "I can't really talk on that abstract level right now," they said.

"It's not abstract, though," I pressed. "If you just stopped for a minute, you'd see that maybe the reason we're in such a minority within the Asian American community is we haven't figured out how to address them. Maybe it doesn't diminish the grief around losing Akai Gurley to also acknowledge their hurt, to ask what the hell is going on that they're pouring out for Liang."

"Let me know how it goes on the other side."

I winced and thought about arguing but instead muttered a goodbye.

Tiff's accusation pained me because it was the same one I'd wielded against myself for so long. The two of us had shared a furious energy, an exacting conviction, but now I saw what fueled it and knew I'd have to stop—I no longer believed in my guilt.

* * *

I sat outside CJ's apartment and watched her walk toward the car in her hurried slouch. She slid into the passenger seat. "'Suup," she said.

"Thanks for meeting up," I said.

"For sure."

I drove and held back my flood of apologies. "You still like KCRW, right?" I asked. I tapped on the radio as a consolation gesture, a nod to our perennial argument in high school: I wanted to listen to my "old man music"—the jazz station—while CJ wanted to play her mellow electronica.

"For sure," she repeated. She rummaged through her bag and started rolling a joint. We were in the same scene as that first night, just four days earlier, but a world had risen up between us.

"You should light," I said. "My mom can tell no matter what."

CJ didn't need a second encouragement, and with a swish of her lighter singed the tip and exhaled through her nose. She reclined her chair a few degrees and her gaze relaxed.

"Let's go to the beach," she said.

I nodded and merged onto the 10 freeway. The air rushed through the windows as we picked up speed. A few cars zipped by, pushing ninety. The freeway at night was a lawless zone—no amount of speed counted against that infinite sheet of pavement.

We came to the end of the 10, where the freeway's long journey from Florida ended and it morphed into a highway up the coast. It was the end of America's promise to let you speed from one end of the country to the other, to remake yourself overnight in a different state. Here was the finish line, the drop away into the ocean, the end of the destiny man- ifest. And once America had bloomed bloodily through this continent, a restlessness settled in, and it pushed forward across the ocean, taking the Philippines and Hawaii, launching its armies into Vietnam and Korea, resulting in, among other things, CJ and me driving in a Toyota with our fucked-up histories.

The ocean spray filled the car and I could taste the water's brine. The breeze cleared the smog away and we could see all the way to the Mal- ibu hills, dotted by the lights of mansions climbing down to the black Pacific.

I turned left into a parking lot and CJ and I got out. The two of us moved by instinct, in silence, crossing the boardwalk onto the beach. We paused, took off our shoes, and stuffed our socks into the heels.

Our pace slowed as our feet sank into the cold sand. The crash of the surf became louder, and the white crests of the waves appeared, illuminated by city light behind us. CJ plopped into the sand, butt first, and hugged her knees. I sat next to her. She took out the half joint she'd saved and I leaned closer and cupped my hands as she lit it.

"Listen," I said as I puffed, the familiar cloudiness slowing my thoughts. "I was being ridiculous the other night. I wanted to be better than someone, anyone. I'm sorry."

CJ sat there, a bemused statue. "Word," she muttered. "I hate that number-one-radical act."

I nodded. The words pained me but felt necessary, like scraping out an infection. "You're gonna say 'I told you so,' but—I can't get behind Tiff's politics anymore."

"I told you so." She considered what else to add. "Bitch."

"Yeah. I can't unsee all the fucked-up things this system does to people, and now I can't unsee the shit my parents told me about what they went through. The two are blurring my vision."

CJ puffed philosophically on the joint. "You know, the time you did the most for me was in high school, when my umma was in the hospital and I was going through my shit."

I thought back to that string of afternoons when I picked up CJ outside Kaiser Sunset and we hotboxed the car, drove to In-N-Out, and wolfed down our Double-Doubles and Animal fries in the parking lot, thinking that nothing would ever taste as exquisite. "All I did was, like, hang out with you."

"Yeah, dumbass. I needed someone dependable to just be there. I was about to lose the one person in my family, even though she's fucking nuts. You probably never understood that because you had your

Brady Bunch–ass family. You did the same when I had my breakdown at Harvard. You always think people want some heroic shit, some big radical act. But just being there, without your head in your ass, without some agenda—that's the most helpful thing." CJ shook out her limbs and smacked my arm. "Blah! That shit's hard, and I know I haven't always been solid like that either. Apology accepted."

I breathed in the salt air. It was, I realized, a perfect night. I'd leave all this the next day for a sludgy April in the city, hustling down slippery subway steps to breathe in the thick condensation that formed in the train. A few days ago, I felt I couldn't take this time away from my important life in New York. Now I saw how much I'd needed to be here.

"Can I see?" said CJ. She nodded to my leg.

I rolled up my pant leg and used my phone to illuminate the scrape. It had turned a gaudy red, emanating clouds of dark blue and purple.

"Fuck," she said in appreciation.

"It's just a flesh wound, like they say."

"I heard you called Jane a bitch."

I blushed. "That was bad," I admitted. "But how can you stand it? Not just the racism but all of K-Town: the gossip, the meanness, the materialism, all that?"

"Because," she said, her voice rich with respect, "Koreans are crazy motherfuckers, and so am I."

"*I'm* not," I blurted.

CJ hocked and spat. "Uh? You're having a nervous breakdown over some cop you don't know, and you're going to *drop out of college* because of him?" She started to count points on her fingers. "You don't know Korean people or history, but somehow you're going to be a 'good ally'? You didn't know your own umma's story until two days ago and you're acting like it's some deep burden you have to carry?" CJ collapsed back on the sand. "You're fucked in the head."

A dozen rebuttals started to form: *It's called organizing, neoliberalism is all a nervous breakdown, dropping out is an act of resistance.* But I couldn't voice any because I knew she was right.

"I'm going to have to think about this."

"Don't, actually."

I relaxed backward too. My mind, which had always been the one part of me I trusted, had become my prison. I closed my eyes and felt the cool sand hold me, let the roar of waves overpower the droning of my thoughts.

"Enough about my shit," I said. "What do you want to do, for once?"

CJ bit her lower lip and the corners of her mouth curled. "Swimming high is amazing."

I looked nervously at the dark water. "But we don't have towels, or even swimming trunks."

She heaved herself to her feet. "Don't pussy out."

"'Pussy out'?"

"If you say 'that's problematic,' I will kick you in the nuts." She walked toward the water and I followed. The beach dipped down, and my feet found the firm sand packed down by waves. Sea-foam crawled onto the shore in wild whorls and I shivered as it slid across my ankles.

"How are we doing this?" I asked, trying to hide my alarm.

CJ laughed. "Get over yourself. We've seen each other."

She stripped off her shirt and bra and wiggled out of her skinny jeans. I looked away and peeled off my bomber jacket and dropped my clothes in a pile on top of it. There it was again, my body, the plain, awkward fact of it.

"Let's go, motherfucker!" CJ whooped and ran into the waves. Her body became a blur against the dark water. She crashed against the churning tops then knifed into a wave. The round shape of her head bobbed up. "Fuck! That's cold."

"I told you!" I ran forward. Water skimmed my ankles, and then splashed against my legs. I dove into the heart of a wave. The sound of the world stopped, cut by the water's hush. The wave wrapped me in an icy sheet, pricking my skin alive. The weed, though, formed a layer between me and the water, softening and brightening all the sensations.

I came up for air. "This is amazing!" I shouted over the water, over the blood ringing in my ears.

CJ laughed and I swam with her beyond the wave break, parting my little slice of the ocean. We waded, backs down, staring at the dark blanket above, streaked by faint clouds. A few bold stars pierced the city glow. CJ yelled. I yelled. We had nothing else to say, no words for the sky or waves or each other. We were just bodies, carried by the swell.

XVII

I WALKED UP TO THE DINING ROOM
table, energized from a heavy sleep. "It's not that hard to get off academic
probation," I announced. "I'll finish my degree."

My parents stared at me with yogurt, berries, and the *L.A. Times*
spread in front of them. Dad slumped back in relief and Mom eyed me.

"We think that's a *very* good decision," said Dad, trying not to appear
too eager. "The revolution will be there when you finish."

"I suppose if it came sooner," I said, "that would be a good thing."

He folded up his section and said he was off to work. He was wearing
one of his identical gray suits that, when I stood to hug him, smelled like
dust and my childhood. He walked out the door.

I sat down across from Mom and she faced me as if it were now time
for business. Her stare was like a heat lamp, and I felt I'd catch flame if I
didn't speak.

"I'm sorry," I blurted. It came out as a croak and I cleared my throat
to try again. "I wasn't actually listening, the other day, about the Coalition. I was being arrogant, like I knew what you should've done." Blood

pulsed through my head, urging me on. "I really respect what you did under the circumstances. I have no idea what that took."

Mom thrummed her fingers on the table. "I told you on the first day this wasn't some lesson for your friends," she said bluntly. "But you kept asking like I was supposed to have some perfect answer, like we knew what the fuck we were doing back then."

"We don't know what the fuck we're doing, either," I admitted. "Or at least, I don't."

We stared at each other, our limitations laid out before us as an invisible centerpiece.

"I remember what it was like to be in the middle of a campaign," said Mom, "to stay on course no matter what."

"Yeah, I'm not even doing that anymore. I just fought with Tiff about it."

"You'll be fine," Mom scoffed. "The shit we went through back in the day? One time, I said something Bobby didn't like at a meeting, and he came to my cubicle afterward and started yelling, *What the fuck! You don't know shit about this country, why don't you learn some better English?* I mean, screaming, with foam on his lips.

"I froze for a second. But you know your mother: after he finished I started screaming back: *Fuck you! Don't you ever talk to me like that!* Everyone in the office peeked over their cubicles at me, because Bobby had gone off on everyone at some point and they were afraid of him."

"Wow," I said. The story doused all my warm images of their Black-Korean duo.

Mom shrugged. "After a while it became a routine. We'd scream at each other, get it all out, then laugh about it the next day."

"That sounds healthy."

"Who said it was healthy? Years later, he learned he had bipolar, and I went to therapy for my anger issues. But we didn't have all that mental health language then. Anyway, with Koreans, you're not really friends until you draw blood." She said this as if it were a brag.

I managed a smile as I thought about the wound running up my leg.

Mom insisted on driving me to the airport and we loaded up the car. She took La Cienega, a name that means "the bog," and I looked out the window at the urban swamp—the windowless Masonic temple and the Thai chicken place with its flaming logo and the lime-colored motel with a jumbo arrow pointing inside. The city's ugliness made room for everything.

Mom nodded toward the back seat. "Last chance," she said.

I turned around and saw Halmoni's white box. I picked it up and held it in my lap. I was inheriting this teapot whether I wanted it or not. "Don't be mad if I damage it with my reckless friends," I said.

"Better to use it once and break it than to stash it away forever."

I opened the box and on top of the teapot sat the photograph of Haraboji, looking up at me with his winner's grin. I shut the lid as if trying to stopper a curse. "Is that a joke?"

"No," said Mom. "You don't have to put it above your bed or anything. But you should know where you come from."

I gritted my teeth. "From an abuser and the woman who let him back into her life? Both of them obsessed with money and status?"

We stopped at a red light. Mom narrowed her lips. "You asked how I felt after Halmoni died and I couldn't answer. It hit me, when I was talking to the abbess, that I don't know if I ever saw Halmoni sad. Ever. Because if she had admitted her sadness, it would've taken over her life. So she never let it in."

"And the abbess told you to feel it," I said.

Mom nodded. "It made me remember how Halmoni grew up wealthy, how her family fled to Manchuria when the Japanese were fucking up Korea, and by the time the occupation was over they'd lost everything.

So she believed that all she needed was a rich husband, or a successful daughter, or a lottery ticket, and she'd get her life back.

"And Haraboji—he was born in the North, then went south for his education. His parents sent money to an uncle to take care of him, but that uncle ran off with the money and the war broke out and America divided the country and Haraboji never saw his family again. So these angry, bitter, materialistic people—when you look at where they came from, why they were like that, it's no wonder."

I swallowed and my chest ached with a quiet, insistent pain. "So what?" I said. "We feel bad for them?"

Mom became very still and upright. "You know, Koreans have this word *hwabyung*, 'burning sickness.' It's when you have so much anger, and it's so repressed, that it destroys you. Halmoni would've rather held on to all her anger toward Haraboji, or me, or Korea, or America, than let go of her fantasy life. When I was an organizer, I was so good at tapping into that anger, getting up in front of people and stoking that fire in them. But then it made me sick, and L.A. burned, and I wondered what the hell it was for. I see the same anger in you, Reed, this feeling like everything in the world is wrong. I see it eating you."

"We have reasons to be angry," I said.

"Of course we do," said Mom. "But you can't go back and change things. You can't ask for a different life."

That was what I wanted, though. What else was the revolution but to go backward and forward at once, to build a future so different that it undid the past? And if we didn't have that, then all we had was the present—this family and country, this life, exactly as they were.

I heard a ragged, wheezing sound. It was my own throat, gasping against the constriction in my chest.

"Honey?" Mom asked in a worried voice.

I pushed the button to open the window. "Just need some air."

"Reed," Mom said, on the edge of worry and impatience. The car swerved and stopped. She thumped me on the back with the heel of her hand. "Inhale, exhale."

I closed my eyes and placed my palm against my heart and felt that swelling again, pushing outward. But if I cracked it open a hairbreadth, I feared it would flood me.

I let go of my heart and focused on inhaling and exhaling, as if my lungs had forgotten what to do, and I needed to teach them.

Mom turned back onto the road. "Keep breathing. We have time before your flight." I heard the nervousness underneath the command. She continued down La Cienega then exited onto a side street. The concrete and stores disappeared. Eucalyptus trees swayed over the road and their sharp, medicinal smell came through the windows. I breathed in more deeply. The road ended in a parking lot that served some scrubby, desert hills.

"Not more exercise," I said weakly.

"You've got to move it out," Mom said firmly.

I didn't have any argument left and followed Mom onto the hiking path. The cement gave way to dirt, and chalky puffs rose around our feet. Prickly bushes with waxy leaves grew out of the sandy earth—plants designed not to be pretty but to retain all the moisture they could in the cruel desert. The incline was enough to make my heart beat faster.

"Better?" asked Mom.

I nodded.

"Reed. What's going on?"

I didn't know what to say and who I'd be once I said it, but I knew I had to speak. "I wanted to create this perfect version of myself," I said. "To be this ideal radical. Because if I could do that, then other people could, too, and we could change the world. Now I come here and find out all this pain I've inherited from generations, from Halmoni and

Haraboji, from the war, the Japanese. Not just our family, but all these Koreans who were abused, then returned that abuse here. Of course they were neocolonizers extracting resources from South Central, of course they climbed onto their rooftops with guns during Sa-i-gu. That's what they knew. Same with these pro-Liang Chinese pouring out: they feel misunderstood, they've never had an outlet to talk about all the humiliation they've endured until now.

"And so now we're just supposed to live inside these forces, these cycles of violence, that we barely understand? That move us around like puppets?" A simple, inane desire came up. "I wish I could cut it all away."

"Yes," said Mom. "But if you did that, who would you be?"

The words hovered around us and I had no answer. The pressure inside me had lightened and I kept following Mom, a step at a time, listening to our feet crunch and slide on the rocky path.

The trail rose along the ridge and we saw the Inglewood oil fields again. The hammerheaded pumpjacks dipped up and down, the silent beasts tearing up the earth, trapped in their dumb labor. It was a brutality that we'd come too far to renounce, and so instead we compromised, driving our fuel-efficient vehicle. We wanted to repair this torn earth and failed and failed and tried anyway.

Mom swung her arms as if to let go of whatever was building in her. "I never wanted to be a mother, you know. After what I grew up with." She spoke softly, and something between a smile and grimace broke across her face. "I digitized our home movies a couple months ago, from that old camcorder. I sat there one night and watched them all: Dad giving you your first bath; you in your Superman pajamas, dancing around the living room; you at your first preschool, singing 'You Are My Sunshine.' You all sounded terrible, so out of tune.

"I sat there and I cried the whole way. Then I watched them again. I cried because I could never have imagined giving birth to someone like that—so untouched by the world. That's when I knew there was something magic that all our politics and theories couldn't explain. That you could come from me."

Mom shuddered, coming back to herself. "Maybe I'm projecting too much happiness onto you. Maybe your crazy-ass mother fucked it up. But at least you know I tried, right? I tried to give you what I didn't have."

A barrier inside me collapsed. It had taken all my life to hear this simple confession, to understand what Mom risked in the primal act of carrying my body in hers. I'd wanted an answer to my questions, wanted to dispel the ghosts of history with the right politics. But the answer wasn't a theory. The answer was my life.

"I know," I said. "You did."

We came to the crest of a hill and stopped. Mom looked up at the powder-blue sky. It faded into a haze at the horizon, and L.A. spread out in every direction, flat and boxy, until cut by the long turquoise arm of the Pacific. A trail of white planes rose in clean lines over the water until they banked toward their destinations.

I looked over at Mom. Her eyes were watering. I blinked. Mine were too. I blinked again and the sun streaked through my tears, the city dissolved into a blur.

"Thank you," said Mom. She reached over to pat my face, and for once, I didn't dodge. "My son."

<<<<>>>>

Acknowledgments

My name is on the cover of this book, but the writing, revision, and publishing of it were done by many loved ones and communities.

Thank you, Mom, for doing the most radical thing I could ask: sharing your stories. The fact that you read and understood this book first means more than anything that comes after.

Thank you, Dad, for teaching me to write, side by side at the keyboard, and to read, next to me at bedtime.

Thank you, Robin, for demonstrating how to come forward as an artist.

My grandparents' spirits shaped this books, especially Dolores Wong, who instilled in me her love of books and libraries, and Jin Hong Lee, whose life set forth a riddle to solve with mine—thank you for the inheritances.

Megha Majumdar, thank you for loving this novel and bringing your energetic eye to every sentence and plotline. Thank you to the Catapult team for carrying this process with care, especially Kendall Storey, Megan Fishmann, Rachel Fershleiser, Kira Weiner, Laura Berry, and Miriam Vance.

Thank you, Julia Masnik, at Watkins/Loomis. I couldn't have asked for a kinder and wiser guide through the labyrinth of publishing.

Rutgers-Newark MFA: Melissa Hartland, Akhil Sharma, Jim Goodman, John Keene, for asking me to think about the praxis of a book; Jayne Anne Phillips, for making me consider every prepositional phrase, Cathy Park Hong, for reading and understanding all the narrator's minor feelings; and my advisor, Alice Elliott Dark, for the immeasurable gifts of always knowing what I was trying to do, and for recommending the exact right books—thank you all. To Sydney Choi for the Chinese-Korean bonding, to Brian Loo for the excellent edits, to Emily Luan for talking food and melancholia, Simeon Marsalis for the long walks and antics, to Như Xuân Nguyễn for the K-pop and sangha, and Lauren Kimiko Parrott for the magical realism.

Thank you, VONA, Virginia Center for Creative Arts, and Summer Programs at Provincetown FAWC for the time, space, and teachers. Thank you, Alexander Chee, for modeling the writing life with grace, Naomi Jackson, for sending fire to my writing hand, and David Mura, for sitting me down to explain how a story works. Thank you, Bushra Rehman, for guiding us through Two Truths and a Lie. Thank you to the late Larry Aubry, cochair of the Black-Korean Alliance, whose work and stories live in this novel.

To the hot pot group: Rob Rusli, Wo Chan, Lara Lorenzo, and Er(ic) Linsker, thank you for community, warmth, and nourishment. To Loma for the tea and boxing. To the Asheville retreat for reading and cheering on an early draft: Nana Duffuor, Kyle Halle-Erby, Harper B. Keenan, Emma Rae Lierly, Han Yu; Sophia Davis and Sowj Kudva, for building and teaching me chosen family.

Thanks to the Asian American arts community, which showed me I'd have readers before I knew I was a writer. Kundiman, for the radically open space, and especially Cathy Linh Che for holding our community with a brilliant heart and mind. To the Asian American Writers' Workshop, especially Jyothi Natarajan and Nadia Q. Ahmad. To Herb Tam and Lu Zhang, Nancy Bulalacao and Ken Leung, Carolyn Antonio, thank you for being my older siblings in this world, and shout-out to Dash and Ava. Thank you, Tomie Arai, for recording and sharing our stories through your art. Thank you, A/P/A Institute at NYU, Amita Manghnani, Laura Chen-Schultz, Ruby Gomez, and Jack Tchen, for the part-time office and library card where I started research on this book.

To the organizers who worked on behalf of Akai Gurley and his family, Cathy Dang, Ruben An, Meejin Seol Richart, Shaun Lin, Aunt T—thank you for teaching me compassion in action.

Susie An, thank you for keeping it real these past twenty years.

To the Zen ancestors, my practice and life are my thanks. To my fellow residents at Ancestral Heart Zen Temple, who held the container that allowed these last drafts to grow: Wesley Simmons Antell, Emme Blong, Carmine Branagan, Ian Case, Julia DeWitt, Camille Goodison, Phoenix Lotus, Kikuko Morimoto, Don Rider, and Inzan Monica Rose Smith. Gratitude beyond words to our teachers: Laura O'Loughlin, whose guidance is as gentle and illuminating as the forest moon, and Kosen Gregory Snyder, who taps the ancient well and shares from it freely.

And finally, thank you, Kaishin Victory Matsui, my best friend. You held my heart with your ocean heart, you heard my voice before I did, you gave me a second chance to be just a kid. I love you forever.

© Beowulf Sheehan

RYAN LEE WONG was born and raised in Los Angeles, lived for two years at Ancestral Heart Zen Temple, and currently lives in Brooklyn, where he is the administrative director of Brooklyn Zen Center. Previously, he served as program director for the Asian American Writers' Workshop and managing director of Kundiman. He has organized exhibitions and written extensively on the Asian American movements of the 1970s. He holds an MFA in fiction from Rutgers University–Newark. *Which Side Are You On* is his first book.